THE
EMPRESS
OF
FIRE

A Novella

BY NED PICKERING

ISBN: 978-0-646-72465-2

Publisher: Ned Pickering Arts

For my own Empress of Fire
Wherever she may be

She is out there
I have to believe she is
My Empress of Fire
Her hands stained with ash and ink
Filled with fire when she thinks
They paint and play and write and weave
A tapestry I can't yet perceive

ONE

Fred sits like a psychedelic Buddha on the couch —
cross-legged, long-haired, holding a Lipton bong with
his old tie-dye T-shirt on and Salamanca Market hippy pants. All around the garage are bohemian hangings and
kooky drawings, oil paintings, and a clutter that goes so deep
you could swim in it.

He leans forward and stares at me with his perpetually
stoned eyes. Fred's forgotten his point — and so have I. He
backtracks now, like always.

"You need someone with more pizazz anyway, Jack. Let
her go, man. Find someone with more fire. Someone respect-
able enough not to cheat. A real empress, like in the tarot
cards."

I open my mouth but he cuts me off with a wave of his
henna-covered hand.

"Forget about her, man."

This is the third time he's said this since I rocked up to his
place this arvo.

"You've got more important things to think about. Like the tarot deck you're making. Just chill, sketch a card, and I'll pack you one."

"How can I forget about her? We dated for like six years, Fred. And the tarot deck is the least important thing. Fair Work isn't doing shit about the café not paying me and Mum is just about to kick me out. I've never seen her so pissed off."

Fred puts down the bong and slowly waves his hands through the air, like he's in touch with some kind of energy field.

"Don't spin out man. The universe will sort you out. If you're strapped for cash I can lend you a buck, but get down to the market with your fiddle and you'll be apples and gravy. You used to play killer sets. What happened to that?"

Fred's always banging on about cosmic shit but he's right.

I shut up and grab the bong off him and he throws me his red BIC lighter — the one with the sticker ripped and safety pulled out.

Exhale. Light. Pull. Shotty.

That's much better.

Fred's watching me and he smiles and nods.

"Better?"

"Mmm."

"You should make a card — *The Empress of Fire.*"

I put the bong back on the coffee table and eye off the tarot card-making stuff.

It's actually a pretty sick name for a card, and she springs to mind — hair like curly red flames, green eyes, deft as a cat.

I'm cutting the card, Fred's finding the aux. Life is good again – until I have one fatal idea.

The Card-Cutter.

Isn't that a cool idea for a tarot card?

I haven't done a self-portrait in years, but I do one now. Me in my current state.

A wonky face with stoned eyes. White paint pen on black card. At the bottom I write: *'The Card-Cutter.'*

I laugh at it, Fred looks over, then I sigh, remembering the shitshow that's the current state of my life.

I take up the scissors in frustration and cut the tarot card clean in half.

The card-cutter cut himself from the deck.

"What's that, man?" says Fred.

I hold up the pieces so he can see, and smile.

"The Card-Cutter cut himself from the deck."

"No, no, no. Why would you do that?"

"What?"

"Nah man, that's like super bad juju. You don't cut yourself out of the deck."

I mock his mysticism. "*Ooo,* something really bad will happen to me."

The garage light flickers uncannily and Fred shakes his head.

"Nah man this is serious shit."

"What could possibly happen?"

Fred doesn't reply — his eyes just go wide staring at something behind me.

The temperature plummets and a chill locks my neck. I try to turn my head to see what Fred is looking at but it won't move.

"Fred what is it?"

"Noo," he says, grasping the couch and pushing back into his seat in terror.

I hear the sound of scissors snipping right in my ears, but I can't turn around.

Fred looks more afraid than I'd ever seen him in my life.

"It's… It's y—"

He just points, one shaking hand at me, then to behind me.

"Fred!"

He's paralysed by fear, eyes and mouth wide, body tense, clinging to the couch.

A shadow looms as if someone's standing over my shoulder and my vision shrouds like fog swallowing the River Derwent.

Snip.

My breath catches in my throat.

Snip.

Snip.

Snip.

Shh

Be light on your feet

They're always out there

Always listening

You can hear them where the sound is missing

Sitting in the bottom of the wind

Rustling through the leaves in the pitch black

Always where they don't belong.

TWO

I blink in a labyrinth of sticks and branches. Whether it's morning or dusk, I can't tell. I'm lying on my back like a carcass, mind blank and vision off-kilter. Twilight filters through the gum leaves above and a few small birds flit through the canopy.

I try to remember how I got here and my head splits.

Give yourself a minute, mate.

Must be hungover, dreaming or dying. I surrender to all three possibilities and roll over onto a camping mat.

A camping mat?

Fred must've put that there for me.

Hang on a second.

Who the fuck is Fred?

I bolt upright. Now I'm really spinning out. I can't remember a single thing. You'd think if I blacked out on the piss I'd feel worse, wouldn't you?

I scratch my head.

Give yourself a minute J—

What?

I can't remember my own name?

I shake my head. *What a wig out.*

In the low light I fumble around and find a backpack, and wriggle round so there's room to tip it out on the camping mat.

A wallet, a box of Redhead matches and a BIC lighter.

Sparks but no darts — must've smoked 'em all last night.

That's when I hear something off-putting.

It sounds like a wallaby fucking around in the undergrowth but what I'm hearing is all wrong.

There's static when I really listen, and in the very bottom of the sound there's something missing.

The sound is missing in places.

I call out through the chaos of Tassie natives. "Who's there?"

A dog barks in the distance. An engine echoes through the bush and nearby foliage crinkles and crackles in the most wrong way.

I grab the lighter, stand up and spark it, but it barely does anything.

I turn my head, trying to lock onto the sound but it's like it's everywhere.

It's like it's inside my head.

And then I see him.

A tall man wearing a hat and sunglasses standing dead still, only a stone's throw away.

He's staring at the flame of the lighter and the reflection dances on his black glasses.

"You right there, mate?" I ask with as much bravado as I can muster.

The man just twitches up, goes all shaky and drops something, then he turns around and disappears into the bush.

The fuck?

By now there's more light. It must be morning.

This must be a dream.

Flicking the lighter lets me find what he dropped.

A black card. I turn it over.

Hand-painted in white paint pen is a tarot card for *Death*.

The wind rustles through leaves in an autumn lane, shown with curled lines. There are faces in the trees with morbid expressions.

What kind of sick joke is this?

I look around again, but no one is there. It's just me.

Trying to remember what happened is useless.

I open the wallet looking for answers. There's only one card in it — a Tasmanian driver licence.

Only it's all wrong.

The picture is blacked out and the letters and digits are all misprinted, stacked on top of each other in a way that's impossible to read.

What a headfuck.

I open the box of Redheads and there's only one lonely match left, except it's burnt at the wrong end.

Did I do that?

I almost chuck it away but it seems like bad luck. I just put the whole box and wallet in the pocket of the Kathmandu jacket I'm wearing.

I wish I knew where I was, but at the same time I can't be too far from civilisation.

I try shake the dreamlike daze but it's no good. I can't remember what happened last night. I can't even remember my own name.

Come on mate, you've ended up in sillier places before.

With that thought, I pick my way through the tangle of branches towards the light.

For a good while I stumble through the native Tassie bush, until I hit a muddy track. The path winds through gum tree and sheoak, running parallel to a wire fence covered in cow tags. It must be the border to someone's property and without a better option I climb over.

A bell chimes in the distance and a kookaburra cackles in the trees above me like it knows.

I'm lost mate, trespassing's fine.

Pushing through the bushes lands me in a clearing of blade grass. Through the gaps in the foliage I can see Kunanyi looming.

Never have I been so glad to see that mountain. Judging from the angle I'm up in the hills of South Hobart.

The sound of someone walking catches my attention and I turn to see an old man striding down the slope.

His long grey beard swings to and fro and he looks completely mad — not angry, just in the way he's dressed.

His knitted hat is full of feathers and the bomber jacket he's wearing is plastered with cow tags. About ten different necklaces hang down his chest strung with keys, feathers, leaves, shells and animal teeth.

He trots along on filthy bare feet, with a handful of anklets dangling more trinkets. Most bizarre of all is the long driftwood stick he carries like a wizard's staff, with feathers sprouting from the end covered in pieces of pottery.

He catches sight of me and stops dead. We stare at each other and his eyes narrow.

Then all of a sudden he's waving the stick through the air furiously, like he's warding off a demon.

"Back! Back!" he yells.

This can't be real so I don't move or react, which seems to perplex him and he stops waving the stick and just squints at me curiously.

"You're not one of them?"

The fuck is he on about?

"One of *them?* One of *who?*"

The man frowns, glances around, then leans in slightly. He lowers his voice with one hand at the side of his mouth and his eyes go wide with fear.

"You know — *one of the others.*"

"What do you mean? Who are *'the others?'*" I say using air quotes.

He waves his stick at me. "Shhh! They're listening. *Always listening.* What are you, an idiot?"

"Who are *they?*"

He mouths a word and I understand.

Death.

I think back to the man in the bushes and the *'Death'* card in my pocket. A chill crawls down my spine like an icy spider.

I shake my head.

"This can't be real."

The old man's eyes bulge in terror. "Don't go mad. That's how they get you. *I've seen it.*"

As crazy as the old man appears, his words and the look in his eyes do make me feel afraid.

"Where am I?"

"Up Strickland Avenue way."

"How did I get here?"

"You tell me."

"I just woke up in the bush back there." I point behind me. "I can't remember a thing."

"What's your name?"

I shrug my shoulders. "Can't remember."

I can tell this is the wrong answer because he starts waving his stick at me again.

"What are you?" he demands, jabbing the thing towards me. "How did you get past the boundary? How did you get past all my charms?"

"Charms? The cow tags?" I shake my head. "Look man, I don't know who I am, where I am, or how I got here. Actually," I add, pulling out the *'Death'* card.

"Did your mate drop this?"

Big mistake.

His eyes go even wider at the sight of it and he cries out, making me jump.

"Bugs!"

With that one word he turns and bolts up the hill like the mad old bastard he is. I've never seen someone that old move that fast.

Bugs?

I look at the card and don't see a single one.

With nothing else to go on, I find myself following.

There upon the grass where he stood, I find another card.

'The Hermit.'

Hand painted in the same white paint pen as the *'death'* card, is a cloaked figure standing in the forest. He holds a lantern high and gazes out at something unseen.

Did that old man really drop this?

And the guy in the bushes before?

This whole thing is whack.

That kookaburra laughs again, like it's mocking me — like it knows something I don't.

Well I can't stay here, so I follow up the hill the way that mad old bastard went.

At the top of the slope the blade grass starts to thin and the gum trees clear. A small, decrepit house squats there, back door to the sagging verandah wide open and no sign of the old man.

I could just leave — find the road and fuck off.

But something isn't right about all this. I want answers.

I climb the back verandah steps, pass some raggedy chairs and stop at the threshold.

"Knock, knock."

Seconds stretch by and I hear nothing but the birds singing their morning tunes.

I feel like I shouldn't, but I go inside anyway.

It's gloomy as hell so I dig the lighter out of my pocket and spark up the flame.

What I see drawn all over the corridor walls can be described as psychotic at best.

Symbols, sigils, heads are scribbled everywhere. Hat and sunglasses, repeated over again in pastel, pen, pencil, charcoal and what looks like blood. There are ambulances with blacked out windows and wonky crosses, paramedics and police, all wearing sunglasses standing around in a big mob. Some of the faces are shown whispering. Some have no faces at all.

It creeps me the fuck out and I have to stop for a second and tell myself this can't be real.

Murmuring starts to leak through the closest door, the handle with mismatched ribbons all dangling from it.

When I shove it open I catch a glimpse of the old man on his knees praying at some kind of altar where a hearth once was.

There are candles, feathers, shells and stones around a central wallaby skull, propped up by driftwood sticks with black cockatoo feathers jutting from its eye sockets and gold wire glinting in its teeth.

The hermit's head snaps toward me and his wild eyes lock onto mine.

He rises with his staff in hand and cries, *"Begone!"* winding it back to hit me.

I slam the door shut and the gust blows the lighter out.

I'm holding it closed in the darkness but he doesn't try open it. I just hear a string of curses and a furious rustling behind the wood that tells me he's tying it shut.

Sparking the lighter again, I let go of the door handle, silently backing away and dipping out through the verandah door.

My heart pounds while I'm going around the house and my head is spinning from all the freaky shit.

Wallaby skulls dangle from the gum trees here and I gasp in the fresh air, not realising I'd been holding my breath.

Looking back, I can't see him following, so I slow my pace going down the driveway.

Then I think of the eerie drawings in the hallway and speed up again.

Where the driveway meets the road, a wire fence has been built.

To keep out *'the others?'*

As I'm vaulting over I notice a torn five-dollar note with a rusty old peg holding it to the wire. Since I have no money, I take it — after all, half a five-dollar note is better than nothing.

Who knows, maybe it'll bring me good luck.

I look down the winding road. From what the hermit said, this must be Strickland Avenue.

Let's get the fuck out of here.

I follow the road downhill, torn five-dollar note in hand and the kookaburra's laughter trailing behind me like a warning.

At first it was just one

Hat and sunglasses, like all the rest

They dropped something and we thought it was nothing

Then they came in droves

"Police! Open up!"

I had never been so afraid in all my life

THREE

Following along the roadside for a few hundred metres, I try to make sense of everything that's happened.

But by the time I hit a Metro bus stop I'm just as clueless as before, and the unease lingers — that kind that makes your stomach clench before something goes wrong.

I sigh and go up to the board. The 449 runs from Fern Tree to Hobart. I've got no idea what time or day it is so I just sit and wait.

While I'm slumped over the bench I wonder if this is a dream again, but really, it's more like a nightmare. Either way, I hope buses still run in nightmares, because walking all the way to Hobart for answers would be a real drag.

I play with the red BIC lighter, sparking it a few times, then taking a closer look at it. The safety's been ripped out like it belongs to a stoner and what's left of the sticker on the back reads: *AWAY FROM CHILDREN… and clothing. Contains flammable gas under… (122°F) or to prolonged sunlight. Never… 005038."*

I've got nothing better to do so I let the flame run.

Then—

I can't breathe.

I kill the flame and cold mountain air rushes back into my lungs. When I spark it up again it's the same thing. No breath while it's burning

What the fuck?

What's left of the barcode has changed.

...004688

It was definitely five-something before.

The number is tied to the gas — and so is my breath. I wonder if I wake up when the lighter runs out?

I'm testing the theory when a Metro bus swings round the corner.

I wave it down and the great beast of a thing screeches to a stop right in front of me.

Hydraulic doors open.

Chuuuh.

I feel uneasy when I see the driver wearing a cap and sunglasses like in the hermit's wall drawings.

I can't see his eyes through the sunnies, but he seems to wave me aboard without even looking at the torn five-dollar note, and before I can finish saying, "Sorry, mate, this is all I have..."

Classic Metro.

What's *not* classic Metro is that everyone on board is wearing hats and sunglasses.

Just like the man in the bushes.

Just like the drawings in the hermit's hallway.

My skin crawls when all their heads turn to look at me. I make my way to the very back seat so none of them can watch me.

There I consider the lighter in my hand again, but don't want to draw attention to myself by sparking it, so I rest it on my lap, take my wallet and pull out the 'Hermit' card.

Fred!

I remember Fred!

His name hits me like a bullet in the back. Memories flood my mind. Fred doing stupid shit in class when we were growing up. Fred teaching me how to identify psilocybin mushrooms. Fred sitting on his couch sparking up a cone with the red BIC lighter.

Fred's lighter — with the torn barcode and ripped-out safety!

I hold it in one hand, the 'Hermit' card in the other, and tears prick my eyes at the memories of my best friend. I can't believe I was wasting the gas.

There, on the backseat of the bus I vow to guard this lighter with my life.

That's when someone gets on the bus that *isn't* wearing a hat or sunglasses.

She's in her thirties, dark-haired, and looks anxious as hell when she sees all the heads turn and watch her walk up the aisle. She carries a leather fiddle case and slides it under her seat, halfway up the bus.

The driver gets us rolling again and I watch as the man sitting across from her, one of *'the others'*, keeps his head turned, staring.

The woman notices, coughs, and jerks her head forward again.

A few seconds go by and she peeks again, finding the man's gaze is still locked onto her.

"What?" she says indignantly, but with a hint of fear in her voice.

The man's fixated on her, completely unfazed by her reaction.

"Stop staring at me!"

She's fully freaking out now and sees that everyone on the bus is staring at her.

Including me.

We make eye contact and I raise a finger to my lips in a 'shh' gesture.

Wrong thing to do.

She freaks out even more, jumps from her seat and nearly falls as the bus slams to a halt.

The woman steadies herself, then darts down the aisle and I notice the ambulance and police car the bus has stopped behind.

Fuck.

I watch it all unfold.

Police and paramedics wearing gloves and sunglasses are waiting for her as she runs out the bus.

They catch her. She's screaming.

I feel sick watching one of the paramedics jab a needle into her arm.

They bring out one of those yellow electric stretcher things, and she cries while a crowd of cops and paramedics engulf her, holding her still and strapping her down.

Everyone on the bus stares straight ahead but me, and it gets rolling again like nothing happened.

Definitely a nightmare.

We go by and I see her eyes full of terror as she's put into the back of an ambulance with blacked out windows.

I press the stop button with a shaky finger. No heads turn.

Thank fuck.

The next stop is at the Cascade Brewery and the bus pulls up near the silos.

As I'm walking down the aisle I notice the woman left her fiddle under her seat and something in me tells me to take it. I figure she won't be needing it where she's going.

I grab it on my way out, not looking back.

But I can hear someone following me.

Trying not to panic, I tell myself it's not real over and over again like a mantra in my head, but it's hard to keep my pace even and get off the bus normally.

Fresh Tassie air slaps me in the face as I step off and start walking down the footpath. There's a truck in the loading zone outside the brewery and in the big rectangular mirror I see not one, but two behind me, cap and sunglasses just like the rest.

My heart races and I can't help but quicken my pace.

I duck down to Cascade Gardens and as I'm power walking along with the fiddle case in hand, I spot what can only be described as a boundary line, just like around the hermit's house.

There right across the path where the entrance to the garden are cairn stone stacks with random items on top of them and others wedged between the stones. There are a few prayer flags, animal skulls, feathers, leaves and other trinkets.

The sight gives me a strange sense of relief and I leap across, continuing down the asphalt under the red leaves of maples.

I take a look back.

The two 'others' walk right up to the cairn boundary line and stop.

They each twitch, as if struck by a sudden shiver, and then their heads jerk up, looking at the sky, then to their sides — anywhere but at the gardens.

I almost laugh as they turn around and slowly walk back up the path.

Maybe the hermit wasn't as mad as I thought.

I watch 'the others' go before walking down into the gardens, autumn leaves dancing through the air around me.

The grass is lush here and I can hear the rivulet flowing to my left.

I spot something on one of the green picnic tables.

Stones are stacked in a pile, decorated with miscellaneous items. I stride closer to see that at the very top a leather-bound book is wrapped in braided ribbons of different sizes and colours, tied up like a net around it with an amethyst crystal sitting on top.

I reach out a hand to pick up the crystal so I can better see the book but stop myself. I don't want to disturb it.

The realisation comes that this is a lot like the altar in the hermit's house and I smile.

Whatever this is, it's connected to the boundary line that's keeping those freaks out — most likely the source of protection.

For a nightmare this is getting pretty elaborate.

I set down the fiddle, sit on the seat and sigh.

Thoughts of Fred come back to me but as much as I try they're fragmented. I just know he would tell me to take this seriously even if it is a dream or whatever.

I put my elbows on my knees and forehead in my hands. I can't help but feel sad. I'm tired from all the anxiety and hungry. As much as I've told myself none of this is real, it's felt real this whole time. I just wish I could remember things. I just wish I could remember my name.

I sigh again and open my eyes. The leather fiddle case stares back at me like it knows I'd forgotten about it.

I guess there's nothing for it but to pop her open and see what's inside.

I flick the clasps one by one and then the lid. Unsurprisingly, a sleek wooden fiddle sits in the green felt.

Too bad I don't know how to play.

I pick it up anyway, and am surprised to find that underneath lies another tarot card.

'*The Axe*' depicts a fiddle with sigils and dots painted on the body in different colours against a black background.

I take the card and fragments of memory hit me like a tonne of bricks.

Mum!

Mum playing the fiddle. Mum making Irish stew. Mum teaching me to play jigs.

I'm overjoyed to the point of tears. Then I remember her crying — crying because of me.

I know it was the last time I saw her.

What were we fighting about?

All of a sudden I'm weeping all over the fiddle in my lap.

I can't remember what we were fighting about. I can't remember her name or what she really looks like.

I can't remember what I look like.

I go on like this for a few minutes, grappling awfully with my amnesia and fragmented memories of Mum and Fred.

Eventually I manage to tell myself that they wouldn't want me to sit here crying and the fact that my memories are actually coming back is consoling.

I realise the point they came back was when I was holding '*The Hermit*' card and, then when I picked up '*The Axe.*'

But why didn't the '*Death*' card restore my memory? And why did '*The Hermit*' only work when I was sitting on the bus?

Some fucking dream hey.

I'm getting pretty hungry now and I have no food. You'd think there would be some people picnicking here I could scum off but there isn't a soul. Traffic goes by on Strickland Avenue but the garden is empty.

I stare down at the fiddle.

I do know how to play.

I take the bow and tighten it. No shoulder rest but that doesn't matter, I just put the horsehair to the strings. What was that tune Mum taught me?

When I try a few notes, my fingers remember for me. All of a sudden I'm playing a waltz — the first tune she ever taught me, only I can't remember what it's called.

The music seems to jog my memory a bit, although it's bittersweet. I remember I used to busk at the markets for a bit of extra cash.

Shit that's not a bad idea.

My stomach is eating itself. With even just a few bucks I could get something to eat.

I'm wondering whether it's the weekend, and if the markets are on, then before I know it I'm packing up the fiddle and heading down the rivulet, on the way to see if the Salamanca Market is running.

* * * * *

Down the rivulet, everyone I pass is wearing a hat and sunglasses even though it's cloudy out.

Fucking weird.

I keep my head down, ignoring them, and they don't turn my way.

The track spits me out into the parking lot of the 'Hamlet' café and I walk past seeing the same thing. All the people sipping overpriced lattes and chewing avocado toast are decked out in hat and sunglasses like it isn't overcast.

Hobart's off too. Walking down Collins Street is eerie with all those freaks about, so I take a right onto Harrington to dodge the crowds — and there's a few out, raising my hopes that it's Saturday morning.

When I get to the intersection at the corner of St David's Park I see the familiar sight of the Salamanca Market bustling but the vibe's completely off. The people all wander around like herds of zombies with hats and shades on.

It's too quiet.

I cut across the park, into the court with the gym and pathology, then out the other side, taking the back way to one of the better busking spots — the one outside Irish Murphy's.

I've realised then that what I'm about to do is probably a really bad idea. Part of me thinks that if I just act like a normal busker no one will notice, another part is hungry, tired of this nightmare, and wondering what will happen to me if I do start busking.

I set that woman's fiddle case on the ground outside Irish Murphy's and pay no attention to anyone as I open it up, tighten the bow, and take the fiddle out.

I chuck the torn five-dollar note in the case for good luck.

A couple heads have clocked me, and I can already feel my heartbeat starting to race. Forcing a deep breath, I remind myself that it's normal for people to watch a busker.

It's fine. Just another Saturday busking at the market.

I quickly check the tuning, then strike up a jig — '*The Mouse in the Cupboard.*'

It's homely. It's pretty, and it reminds me of Mum. The warm feeling freezes over as I look up from the strings.

Every hat and sunglasses head in the vicinity fixated on me.

Fuck.

I don't know what to do but keep playing.

My bow shakes and my sweaty fingers fumble.

I slip up, try cover the mistake by swapping jigs into '*Elanor Neary's.*'

That's when one of '*the others*' wearing full black starts pointing at me and I hear this freaky fucking whispering.

It's satanic. Hissing in my skull, scaring the shit out of me and making me choke.

I do something I've never done in my life.

I drop the fiddle.

It smashes on the asphalt and the pieces fly everywhere.

I'm glancing around like a maniac looking for somewhere to run to, but they're everywhere, all staring and the one that pointed is slowly walking towards me.

A red-headed girl darts forth at me, her sunglasses falling from her face.

Wide-eyed and deft as a cat, she snatches up the torn five-dollar note from the case and a leaf that must've blown in, stabs through both with a sewing needle and thread, then pins it to the lapel of my jacket.

She does all this fast as lightning while I stand there stunned, thinking I'm about to die.

"Quick!"

She grabs my hand, pulling me into Irish Murphy's so forcefully that I almost fall over.

All of *'the others'* in the pub stare as the red-head pulls me left, through the back taproom and straight up a flight of stairs near the bathrooms.

She opens the door at the top and shoves me inside.

I turn back in a daze to see her slam the door shut, and yank something bizarre from her pocket

It's like a madman's rosary, made from a deck of cards with binder clips on each side. Rings dangling from their metal ends and a loop of braided ribbons is strung through one of the binder clips, which she uses to hang it on the doorhandle.

She goes still once it's on, sighing loud and deliberately.

Then she turns around and slaps me straight in the face.

"What the fuck do you think you're doing! You dickhead!"

My cheek burns and I stumble back while her big green eyes stare at me with the intensity of a furnace.

She raises a hand to hit me again and I preventively flinch.

This makes her stop, then laugh like music.

"Fuck, sorry. But what... what was that? They hate music, and no charms or talisman — what are you, suicidal or something?"

The hermit flashes through my mind, all covered in trinkets like he just crawled out of the tip, and I notice the girl in front of me has multiple necklaces on, just like he did.

"Charms?" I mumble, sounding like a bloody idiot.

She exhales sharply and rolls her eyes. "Don't you know *anything?*"

I hold my hands up in surrender.

"No?"

She laughs but I don't know what's funny, I'm just struck by how scary and beautiful she is.

"Ohhh. You just got here, didn't you? Where did you start?"

Not a dream. Not a nightmare.

"I woke up in the bushes. Up Strickland Avenue. What's going on with everyone? What happened to Hobart?"

Her eyes widen and the corners of her mouth curl up.

"You made it all the way *here* without knowing anything? Sit and listen boyo."

She pushes me back, but I step past her when I spot another tarot card on the floor behind her.

'The Empress of Fire.'

A woman floats with flames all around her, red hair scrawled in paint pen.

I hold the card and my head spins as the memories come back — Fred sitting on the couch with a bong in his hand.

"A real empress, like in the tarot cards."

I was making tarot cards. I was going to make that card.

I turn and see that the girl next to me *is* the Empress of Fire, and I think she realises it too because she's staring intensely at it with those big green eyes of hers.

"Did you drop this?" I ask.

She looks at me differently now and I can tell she's thinking hard.

"Sit."

I pull up one of the spare chairs in the room. She does the same and reaches into her jacket pocket.

"This is you, isn't it?" she says, holding up a tarot card that's been cut in half.

I can't see what the picture is but the bottom reads: *The Card-Cutter*, and when I take it the memories hit me as hard as the slap in the face I just got.

"Ohhh… What. The. Fuck."

I can almost hear Fred's voice.

"Nah man, that's like super bad juju. You don't cut yourself out of the deck."

Something was behind me. I couldn't look. Then I blacked out and woke up in the bush? In this fucked up version of Hobart?

"You cut yourself from your own handmade deck, didn't you?"

I look up to the Empress and can only nod.

"Pass me mine."

When she takes it she goes very still, staring down at the *'Empress of Fire'* card in her hand. A tear breaks out of one eye, and she hastily wipes it away.

"What is it?"

She looks over to me slowly and speaks like she can't believe it. "I really did burn my deck."

"You burnt your own handmade tarot deck?"

She nods. "That's why I haven't been finding any cards. It's probably why I don't have a tether either."

"A tether?"

She looks at me like I'm stupid again and says, "What did you wake up with?"

"Some random stuff."

She shakes her head impatiently, red hair swaying side to side. "Show me."

I empty my pockets, the wallet, and lay the items on the floor — Fred's lighter, the matchbox, the blacked out driver licence, and the tarot cards: *'Death,'* *'The Hermit,'* and *'The Axe.'*

"I found the tarot cards along the way."

I watch her stare down at them, narrow her eyes at the cards, then pluck up the *'Death'* card and hold it to her ear.

She frowns, then passes it to me. "This one's a bug."

"A bug?"

It looks just like the others to me. But for the first time I notice it feels cool in my hand.

"If they can't get at you they'll try plant a bug. Listen."

I put it up to my ear, hear nothing at first, then a really quiet whispering, like when that one of 'the others' wearing all black pointed at me.

"It's whispering. What else does it do?"

"Weakens protection. If you've got no charms or anything it'll slowly draw them in. Enough bugs inside a boundary and the shrine is useless."

I pass back the bugged *'Death'* card, and she rips it into pieces before picking up the blacked-out driver licence and holding it up for me to see.

"This is your real *'Death'* card. This is what will happen to you if they get you."

"The hat and sunglasses people?"

She nods.

"What are they?"

"Death. Dead people. Some types are worse than others. Worst of all are the Faceless Ones."

"The Faceless Ones?" I ask, remembering the picture of one in the hermit's corridor while a shiver goes down my spine.

"They're rare. They only come when you destroy one of the shades."

"The shades?"

"That's just what I call them — the hat and sunglasses people."

"And you destroyed one? Like killed them?"

"Not me, someone I knew."

I can tell this is painful for her by the way she changes the subject, saying "What else you got?" and picking up Fred's lighter.

She turns it over, sees the ripped sticker and torn out safety. "This is your tether, isn't it?"

"It's my best friend Fred's lighter. What do you mean by tether?"

"It's your tie to the real world. If it's destroyed or taken by the shades you die and can never get back. Everyone's tether is different. Some can offer protection or be used as weapons. I'm guessing they don't like looking at the flame, or the fire could kill them. Double edged sword though."

"Why?"

The Empress just looks at me. "It still runs right?

"Yeah but I can't breathe when it's running."

The Empress blinks. "You haven't been wasting it have you?"

"Not since I remembered it was Fred's."

"Good. Don't use it unless you have to."

"Why?"

The Empress passes it back and stares me in the eyes. "When that lighter runs out you die. You can never go back home. Fred probably dies in the real world too."

I stare down at the lighter. "How do you know all this?"

"Someone taught me but they got taken. I've been here three months and I don't know if I'll ever get out. I've got no tether and I haven't been finding any cards cause I burnt my deck."

"You found my card. Well, half of it."

"I think that's different."

"How?"

"I don't know. I don't know everything."

"Where did you find it anyway?"

"Started with it — like all this," she gestures to the items on the floor.

She's quiet for a second, with that thinking look on her face. Then she asks, already reaching for it, "What's in the matchbox?"

I say nothing as I watch her open it, take the only Redhead match out, burnt at the wrong end.

She's staring at the red phosphorus tip in her fingers, eyes wide, slowly smiling, then grinning from ear to ear.

The Empress of Fire leaps out of her chair and hugs me with enough force to knock me over chair and all if it weren't for her arms around me.

I think I fall in love then and there and I can't say why.

I'm completely bewildered as she pulls back, holding my head in her hands with an electric look on her face.

"This is my tether! Your name is Jack! Isn't it?! Tell me it is?!"

I'm astonished — she's right! Now I'm grinning back at her too. It feels fucking good to know my name again.

"But how do you know?"

"I just do! Do you know mine?! Tell me!"

I can only shake my head, and this visibly dampens her spirits, making her remember herself. She lets go of me and sits back down.

"What should I call you?"

She looks down, looks sad, and I don't like seeing it.

"My friend called me Ally. I started in an alleyway."

"Ally," I smile. "I like it. Thank you for saving me Ally."

She gives me a smile back.

"What was that you did though — with the note and the leaf," I say, holding the thing up, still dangling from my jacket.

"It's a charm. To help protect you."

"I've seen them before. This crazy old man was covered in them. How does it work?"

She waves a hand. "Synchronicity, quantum-entanglement. I don't know how to explain it properly, but you can read about it. Basically, certain items appear that you're drawn to, or maybe you start with a couple. They're called charms and they help protect you from shades. Once you've seen a few they're easy to spot."

"And it works the same for boundary lines? And shrines? And what's that you put on the door then?"

She puts her palms together and I can tell she's about to do some serious explaining.

"It's sort of the same but different. The thing on the door is called a talisman. It's made from an item of particular signif- icance — usually someone's tether. In this case, it's my friend's incomplete deck, some binder clips, and a bunch of different rings and ribbons I found. It's way stronger than a charm. If you act normal while you're holding it the shades won't even look at you."

"Now, a shrine is basically a stationary talisman, but with way more items. You put a boundary line of charms around it and it'll protect the area. The shades won't cross over unless it's damaged or bugged."

"There's one in Cascade Gardens," I say and she's grinning beautifully again.

"I made that one!"

Something about her happiness is infectious, so I'm smiling back at her. "What's the book at the top?"

The corners of her mouth drop.

"A Carl Jung book."

"Your friend's?"

Ally nods.

"Sorry."

"Don't mention it," she replies, and I take the words seriously, changing the subject.

"So I go back to the real world if I get all my cards?"

"Cards, memories, usually your name — but you've already got that. Hey, what were you doing busking anyway? And where did you get your fiddle? Did you start with it?"

"A woman on the bus had it, but she got taken. I saw the whole thing. I thought I was in a nightmare." My stomach rumbles. "I was busking because I was hungry and didn't have any money."

"Except the torn five-dollar note. But you didn't start with that?"

I laugh. "After I started I stumbled into a boundary line — this crazy old man's one up in Strickland Avenue. He thought I was a shade when I showed him the bugged '*Death*' card and bolted to his shrine. When I crossed the boundary to leave I took the note from it."

"The Hermit of Strickland Avenue," nods Ally. "I've heard about him, heard he's mad as hell. You should be really careful of other survivors Jack. There are renegades out there who hunt people for their stuff — tethers, charms, talismans, food — anything that's useful. They're seriously bad. If you ever see a car covered in charms, get the fuck out of there."

"I will avoid any charm-covered cars. But speaking of getting the fuck out, what do we do now? There's no shrine here. Will that talisman keep us safe? I'm starving."

"I'm not staying here. And no, the talisman won't keep us safe. It's a strong one but look —" Ally points to the door. "In the side."

Wedged between the door and the frame I can see part of another card sticking out.

"Definitely a bug," says Ally. "They'll pile up until the talisman is weakened enough for them to get in. Here," she reaches into her pockets and pulls out a pair of sunglasses. "I have a spare pair for you. I'll pick up mine on the way out."

"Does that work?"

"I think it helps us blend in. Or at least it makes me feel safer. But we can both hold my talisman until we get home."

"Is it safe out there?" I ask, and Ally goes over to one of the windows and peeks through the curtain.

She beckons me over. "Come look, Jack."

I peer down at the market. There's shades everywhere, even more than before.

"They're drawing in after all that commotion," says Ally. "I bet there's a pile of bugs on the other side of the door too. We probably don't have much longer."

"We need to go. *Now.*"

Walls burning

Death is a whispering liar

How do I get out

Of my labyrinth of fire?

FOUR

Ally takes the talisman off the door and entwines the braid of ribbons through my fingers, then hers, and holds my hand which I quite like. Hers is warm which is no surprise really.

"Ready?" she whispers, and I nod.

She opens the door and points down to a pile of trinkets on the floor — a cracked watch, a bent spoon and a broken pint glass — among others.

"Bugs, see?"

I nod and we step over them, carefully going down the stairs.

Halfway down Ally freezes when a shade comes to the bottom of the flight. They're holding something — another cracked glass, and their head starts to turn toward us but then stops. They twitch a little, then turn around and shuffle off.

I smile at Ally and she squeezes my hand.

Shades crowd the taproom of Irish Murphy's, even more than before, but none of them look at us while Ally guides me through by talisman-entwined hand.

Outside they mill about the market like droves of zombies in the cold Tassie air. I'm afraid but Ally isn't. She leads me to where I dropped the fiddle and crouches down, taking her fallen sunnies and the broken head of the instrument dangling with strings.

With a wink she puts her sunnies on and whispers, *"This way,"* taking me up the same hill I walked down.

"They can't see us, can they?"

"It's a strong talisman. You saw how many bugs they put at the door. Just keep an eye out for uniformed ones — we're lucky it's a Saturday, there's less people working."

We've hit Sandy Bay Road now, and that's when we hear the sound of a car hooning.

"Renegade," whispers Ally, yanking me by the hand behind a car in the Harcourts carpark.

"Get down, quick."

We hit the deck, gritty concrete under our bellies while we watch the road through the bottom of one of those soccer mum cars.

A Mitsubishi Lancer with dodgy paint and tinted windows screeches up Sandy Bay Road and it's covered in charms — skulls, animal teeth, black feathers and the cracked sunglasses of shades attached all over.

It does a massive skid and disappears up the street.

I glance at Ally and she's all tense, more afraid of this renegade than she's afraid of the shades. We hear sirens coming up the road and a cop car zips past in pursuit.

"Shit! I hope he didn't clock us!" says Ally. "Not this close to my place… *renegade bastard*. We need to get out of here. The shades will be all stirred up after seeing that. Up."

We rise together and I dust myself off with my free hand, by now the other is sweaty as hell, entwined with Ally's hot hand and her talisman.

We power walk up the road in silence and cut through Alberta Street, and then into Fitzroy Place.

"It's up here," says Ally, and soon she leads me through the gate outside one of the houses and I see the boundary line running on the inside of the fence.

Clever — out of sight from the renegades.

The house is a derelict two storey with paint peeling in flakes and ivy choking every bit of it.

Ally lets go of my hand with the talisman and produces a key, opening the faded red door with a creak.

"This is home."

I smile and step through the threshold after her, the floorboards groaning under me.

Inside is nothing like the outside. There are patterned hangings all over the walls, shells and stones on the furniture, and the living room has been converted into a painting studio with a shrine featuring a cracked teapot on the coffee table.

The work on the easel stares back at me. It's an abstract of fire painted in swirling ash and ink, with cursive writing at its heart that takes me a second to read.

How do I get out of my labyrinth of fire?'

"What do you reckon?" asks the artist watching me.

"It's beautiful — they're all beautiful," I say, gesturing to the rest of the works.

She clearly has a thing for painting natural patterns. There's water, rocks, tree bark, and more painted on smaller canvases all over the room.

"You paint?" she asks.

"I'm not sure," I reply. "I can remember painting tarot cards but I'm not sure about anything like these."

Ally smiles. "Well you can only find out. But come on, let's fix you some food."

She leads me to the kitchen and takes a Tupperware out of the fridge.

"Pesto pasta," she says, seeing me eye it curiously.

"How do you get food here?" I ask as she heats a frying pan and chucks it in.

"Good question. The answer is stealing and finding. If you've got a good talisman you can pretty much just walk into a shade's house and take what you need."

"That easy?"

"No, not really. Too noisy and they notice you. Then they follow you and bug your boundary line. And you want to make sure there's none of all-blacks or uniformed ones home."

I'm reminded of that one at the market. That satanic whispering in my head — it makes my skin crawl just thinking about it.

"What's with them, the ones that whisper? One pointed at me at the market and I heard it right in my ears. Scared the fuck out of me and I dropped the fiddle."

Ally nods as she stirs the pasta. "I saw it. And I don't know exactly. There's something up with them and sound. When it's quiet and they're around. If you really listen you can hear them. It's like they're there in that space your mind can't register."

My eyes widen at the memory of it this morning when I first woke up, and I tell Ally about it, explaining that that's when I got bugged.

"But why couldn't the shade kill me? Why'd it have to leave a bug?"

"Your tether," she replies. "You said you sparked it up."

"Ohh. I'm slow. It makes sense. That whole time I thought I was in a nightmare."

"I woke up this morning from a nightmare."

"Yeah?"

Ally puts the pasta onto plates. "Shades everywhere inside the hospital. I can't really remember it now but I remember it was awful. There was this one with no face..."

"Yuck," I say, then add, "Unlike this. This smells good Ally, thank you."

She grins and hands me a fork. "I like to eat on the balcony."

"Sounds good to me."

The balcony has a good view of the River Derwent, and by now the sun isn't far off setting. Autumn leaves blow in, and when I go to sit in one of the puffy old armchairs I spot a card in the side of the seat.

I point. "Not a bug?"

Ally smiles. "Not a bug — can't have gotten all the way up here."

'*The Sanctuary*' depicts the front of the house, with a couple of the charms of the boundary line visible through the bars in the fence.

I remember home.

A big wooden house by the beach, faceless family all around, Mum's garden full of nasturtiums and tomatoes and seaside daisies.

The vision guts me like a fish. Tears sting my eyes and my throat tightens. I blink and clench my jaw, not wanting to cry in front of Ally. Of course, she notices anyway and puts a hand on my shoulder giving it a rub and squeeze.

"You'll feel better once you've eaten."

Her soft voice and touch make my chest pang with love. I've only known her half a day but there is something about her that draws me in, even if she did slap the shit out of me when she first saved me.

We eat in silence — me thinking about home, her probably thinking about how she can't remember home, how she's probably trapped here forever, how her friend got taken. I don't know, but I can tell she's thinking of something from the way she watches the horizon line so intensely.

We finish our meal like that. The sun dies away behind a hill in the direction we can't see, and Ally turns to me with warmth in her eyes, and a hint of that electric look I saw earlier behind her expression.

"Let me see your tether," she says, and I oblige, taking it from my pocket and handing it over.

I think she's up to something but I'm not sure what. She just turns it over in her hand and smiles.

"Nice stoner lighter."

"Thank you."

"Don't waste the gas," she says, sparking it for a second to light a candle.

"Hey that's my life you're playing with."

Ally's eyes dance with the light of the flame and she grins.

"I saved it. I can do what I want with it. Here."

Her fingers brush mine as she hands back the lighter. The air shifts as the look on her face tells me it was no accident.

"Don't get lost in the memories Jack."

"I won't."

For a second I wonder if I'm dreaming this too.

Then she's already on me, hands, hair, lips and all — hotter than hell.

Ready or not, I am completely lost to her.

* * * * *

We are lying in Ally's bed. She is warm and soft and smells like heaven. I haven't felt this good since I ended up here. Probably since long before that, and I know I've lifted her spirits too. She must have been lonely since her friend got taken.

"Jack, I have a theory."

"Yeah?"

"You started with my tether. I started with half your card. I think... I think if I can help you get back to the real world, maybe I get to go back too."

I can't help but smile at her. "I like that theory a lot."

She kisses my cheek. "There's no real way of knowing, but it's the best shot I have."

"So you'll help me find all my cards?"

She nods her head and curls into me.

"It's been so hard by myself. I almost let them... I almost just let them take me once."

I feel her pain like it's my own and stroke her curly red hair with my free hand.

"You have me now, Ally. Like you said, you saved me — I'm yours."

"Good," she says, and yawns then kisses my dead arm.

Very soon, her breathing changes in that way that tells me she's asleep.

I feel more content than I can ever remember, which is pretty easy when you only have a few memories. All the same, everything about Ally affects me significantly and despite all that's happened today, I drift off easily listening to the gentle sound of her breathing.

*****

The next morning I wake to the smell of food and Ally leaning over me like an excited child, her big green eyes full of light.

"Pancakes," is all she says, giving my arm a pull and then going through the doorway to the balcony.

I crawl out of bed and find her sitting in one of the balcony chairs, a plate of pancakes drenched in maple syrup in her lap and another plate sitting on the coffee table for me.

"Look at this — yum — how long have you been up?"

She grins back at me. "Since dawn. You overslept big time. And it's just one of those homebrand add water and shake thingos, but the maple syrup is proper Canadian stuff."

It tastes amazing. After we eat I suggest we go scouting for cards and Ally agrees, saying we can look for items to make my tether into a talisman at the same time.

"But where to start?" I ask.

Ally runs her fingertip on the plate and licks the maple syrup off it. "Cards usually appear in places of significance. You were playing fiddle, surely one of your cards would appear at the New Syd? There's always fiddle music there."

"That's smart," I reply.

"I actually made a start on your talisman too."

Ally pulls Fred's lighter out of her pocket and I see she's woven strings from the broken fiddle around it like a net with a large loop at the top.

"Ta da!" she smiles, putting it around my neck like a necklace. "You can wear it and still use it if you need to. This way it'll always be within arm's reach and you'll never lose it."

"This is so cool Ally, thank you."

"It needs more though — few feathers, ribbons, animal teeth —I don't know, but it's a start. It won't offer much protection as is, so you'll still have to share mine."

"I don't mind that," I smile. "Even if your hand is warm as hell."

She swats me with one of those hands. "I'm supposed to be an empress of fire, what do you expect? It's not my fault your hands get so sweaty."

Just as she says that a feather blows into the balcony and I manage to jump from my seat and catch it before Ally does.

"That's one!" she grins with that electric look on her face. "Your first one! Congratulations!"

It's white and speckled and I hold it up to Ally smiling.

"A baby seagull feather."

She takes it and I stand there while she fixes it to the necklace made from Fred's lighter, the broken fiddle's strings, and now one juvenile seagull feather.

"It suits you."

I take advantage of our proximity and kiss her to the best of my ability.

"Thank you."

She smiles. "I bet you'll find more today. I just know you will."

Ally is right.

We are walking down Collins Street on the way down to the New Sydney Hotel when I catch another feather floating in the air, almost letting go of her hand and the talisman in the process.

A nearby all-black turns their head, but after we go still for a moment, they carry on walking by.

The second feather is black with a splotch of yellow on it, belonging to a yellow-tailed black cockatoo. And now me.

Ally grins as she fixes it to Fred's lighter around the corner of the Men's Gallery, and we carry on walking.

Arriving at the New Sydney Hotel, I raise my eyebrows at the boundary line around the pub, but Ally shakes her head.

"It's bugged to all hell," she whispers and squeezes my hand. *"Be careful, and follow my lead."*

I nod, and she takes me through the front door.

The taproom is full of shades and at the round tables where the session usually is, one of them plays a distorted jig on a black fiddle, out of key and all wrong, just like the lights. They flicker with static, and I feel a chill even though the hearth is blazing.

Ally leads me through by the hand, navigating so close to the shades that I hear a static in my ears with the same missing sound as when I first woke up.

I'm getting anxious now, and I can feel my heart beating faster as Ally points to the bar where someone's old shrine sits.

But it's all wrong.

The shrine is bugged and even I can tell. Full of cards and broken pint glasses, pieces of instruments and rusty coins.

Behind the wood bartenders mill about in all-black pouring pints. The closest ones seem to tilt their heads at us, almost noticing but not quite.

Ally pulls me against the wall and whispers, *"The bugs make them more sensitive, and look."* She points again.

Tucked next to a bottle of Jameson is another card.

"That's yours Jack, I know it is. Stay still here and they won't notice you. I'll get it okay?"

I'm unsure. It seems dodgy but I trust Ally, and so I nod and hug the wall, holding my lighter necklace at my chest while she takes her talisman from my fingers and moves down the pub.

Between passing shades I watch Ally slip behind the bar, holding her talisman closely. She's deft as a cat, moving around the shades with well-practiced efficiency.

I hear a tap on the wood as a shade adds another bug to the broken shrine — a cracked guitar pick, and it's the last straw.

The lights flicker.

As Ally draws her hand back from the shelf with the tarot card between her fingers, one of the bartenders grabs her wrist.

She screams, yanks her hand back and puts both to her ears, closing her eyes and crying out, "Cass!" while the shades close in around her.

All I can think to do is use Fred's lighter.

I jump up onto the bar and all the shades turn to me.

"Look at this you fuckers!"

I spark the lighter — breath going still in my throat.

The shades all twitch and jerk their heads around as Ally opens her eyes and sees me standing on top of the bar with the lighter burning.

I reach out to her and she takes my hand, climbing up onto the bar.

We run along the wood while shades reach for our legs.

Ally kicks one of their hands away and I boot the broken shrine before jumping down after her. We dart through the door.

Outside I release the lighter, dizzy and breathless.

Ally grabs my hand, putting the ribbons of her talisman in it.

She pulls me up Bathurst Street while I gulp in the cold Hobart air.

Shades on the street turn their heads as we run and more of them pour out of the New Syd after us.

"To Cascade! We can't let 'em bug my shrine!"

We run up the street hand in hand and Ally leads me through the library carpark, only slowing once we're around the corner.

"We act normal now. The all-blacks will still follow us but our talismans will keep them at bay until we get to the gardens."

She knows her stuff. Only the all-blacks follow us up the rivulet, moving in a pack of four and I can hear their broken whisperings as we go.

But they turn away as we cross Ally's boundary line into Cascade Gardens. Each drops a bug on the boundary which Ally kicks away once they leave.

There in the gardens we can finally relax.

We take to one of the park benches, with a view of that big concrete thing the rivulet runs down.

"Who's Cass?"

Ally looks away.

"My friend. The one the Faceless got."

"She's the one that taught you everything?"

Ally nods, watching the autumn leaves fall.

"She found me as soon as I started somehow. I was in the city. I had no tether and no clue — I would have been done-for."

I take her hand in mine and ask, "How did it happen with the Faceless?"

Ally sighs. "We were hunting for cards. It got messy in the Hanging Gardens. Police came. One of them grabbed me and so Cass used her tether." Ally pulls it from her pocket.

It's a small flip knife with a wolf on one side of the handle, and the other side missing.

"Fuck."

"She stabbed the shade and saved me. We thought we were safe back at her shrine, but the Faceless walked straight through the boundary line. It didn't go for me, but I saw it happen."

Ally lets go of my hand and looks afraid of the memory. I can't help but pry more.

"What happened?" I try ask as gently as possible.

She turns to me, big green eyes swimming.

"It stole her face. It made her into a Faceless."

The image in my mind makes my eyes water too, and I hug Ally long and hard there on the bench.

She sniffs, pulls away, and wipes her eyes.

"Hey, what did you say to the shades in the pub anyway? You yelled something but I couldn't hear it over them whispering in Cass's voice."

I smile and hold my talisman up. *"Look at this you fuckers!"*

Ally laughs, which sets me at ease. "I can just imagine all those shades wigging out at you. You saved me, hey, now we're even."

I just smile, and she plants a kiss on my cheek.

"Oh, your card," she remembers pulling it out of her pocket.

'The Flagon' depicts a pint and cigarette on wood. As I take it in my hand, the memories come back, just like with the other cards.

This time it's less painful.

I remember me and Fred and faceless others having good times at different pubs around Hobart — The New Sydney Hotel, Hanging Gardens, Preachers, The Republic.

I'm smiling staring at the card, remembering jokes and drinks and games of pool.

Ally grins at my reaction. "Good times eh?"

I nod. "Good times. I hardly want to let go of this."

"But you have to. You're here, not there. But we'll get you back."

Ally takes the card from my hand and I feel sadness creeping in.

I can't help but sigh and look around at all the fallen leaves.

She puts an arm around me. "I've got you. You'll be able to drink with your mates soon. You've already got a bunch of cards."

"I know," I reply weakly, and rest my head on Ally's shoulder.

She is warm and her hair is ticklish but smells like home. We sit in silence for some time.

But as we soon learn, the peace never lasts. Not for us.

*****

"What now Empress?"

Ally brushes her fingers on mine as I take my head off her shoulder, watching the autumn leaves fall.

"I don't know about you but I'm starving. I say we check this boundary for bugs and bounce. We should do some scavenging on the way home. What I have won't last with you around."

"Are you saying I'm fat or something?"

Ally gives me a shove.

"You're a boy. Boys clean out cupboards. Now be a good one and help me look for bugs."

We leave the park bench and prowl along the boundary line, sifting through cairn stones and prayer flags for bugs. Amongst all the random items I'm not sure what to look for, but Ally starts finding them easily since she put everything here.

She shows me shards of beer glasses, rusty coins, a few fake tarot cards —the sort of stuff that was at the New Sydney.

I get the idea. There's a scratched-up guitar pick with a triskelion on it that makes my fingers numb when I pick it up. I show Ally.

"There you go — you're useful after all." She hands me her collection. "Chuck it all in the river, I'll rip these cards up."

"Yes your majesty."

Ally grins.

With my hands full of bugs I can hear that whispering again and it gives me chills. By the time I get down to the riverbank it's more distinct and I can make out Fred's voice.

"You cut us out Jack... ...We're dead because of you."

The guilt makes me feel sick.

I throw all the bugs into the rivulet and breathe a sigh of relief while rubbing some heat back into my hands.

When I'm going back up to Ally, she's standing at the boundary line watching a shade walk up the path.

It's one of the all-blacks, with a snapped drumstick in hand, and it stops just short of the boundary line when Ally lifts her talisman high

It twitches up and drops the broken drumstick.

The wood clatters on the ground and starts rolling down the path while the shade stares at Ally for a moment before looking away.

As it shuffles back down the path like a zombie, I release a breath I didn't know I was holding.

I reach Ally and she turns to me with eyes wide and sadness behind her gaze.

"It was whispering to you?"

She nods. "Cass's voice again."

"You okay?"

"Yeah. You? I gave you heaps of bugs. Sorry."

"I'm fine. I heard my best mate's voice, but it's fine — chucked 'em all in the river like you said."

Ally rubs my arm. "Come on, let's find something to eat. It's not safe here anymore. Not today. The IGA isn't too far."

We take the top exit out of Cascade Gardens, crossing Ally's boundary out onto the main road. The whispers I heard when I was holding the bugs are still on my mind so I start asking Ally questions while we walk along the footpath.

"Why do the bugs whisper like that? What are they really?"

"I don't really know but I have theories. Cass had theories. They're fragments of memory. Identity gone wrong. They try tempt you to lose yourself in the same way."

I look around the street contemplating. A couple shades get out of a Corolla outside the badminton centre carrying rackets with holes in the netting.

"This whole place though. It's like Hobart but up-side-down. And there's just as many shades as there are people in the real world. They can't all be dead can they?"

"I like that," replies Ally. "Hobart but upside-down. When I said dead people I only meant the stronger ones — the all-blacks, uniformed ones and that. Cass thought the regular ones were just the parts of peoples soul's in the real world that they let die."

"What, like giving up on dreams? Becoming a slave to the system? Not believing in things? Not believing in things like tarot?"

"Identity. Spirit. Past beliefs. Something about it goes backwards when you destroy your own handmade cards."

"It's like something from a book or movie," I say. "Except half the plot's missing — like why do cards just appear? And how do the shades have a sense of where we are even if they haven't seen us?"

Ally nods along. "And why did you start with my tether? And me with half your card?"

"Well I can kinda answer the first part. That day I cut myself from my deck, Fred was telling me I should be with someone more fiery. An Empress of Fire, he said. I was gonna paint your card."

"Huh. So we really are tied together somehow. But I've been here for months. It doesn't make any sense unless time is warped here like everything else."

"Whoever made the rules is smoking some good shit."

Ally stops in her tracks.

"What? You knew I was a stoner from the lighter."

"It's not that," whispers Ally, pointing down the road. "Look. That shade is carrying a bug."

I follow her finger. Outside the Cascade Road Calvary an all-black is walking down the street carrying a tarot card, only its headed away from us.

"There's someone else around," says Ally. "They must already be sitting on a few bugs since we can't even see them."

"What do we do?"

Ally turns to me and her forehead creases. "We help them. Or at least try to. Here." She takes my hand and entwines her talisman in our fingers. "We follow the shade but keep our distance."

The all-black stalks down Cascade Road clutching its bug, then drifts through the intersection without even checking for cars.

Ally raises an eyebrow at me when it goes straight into the IGA on the corner.

"Coincidence?" I say.

"Synchronicity."

I watch more than a few shades going in and out of the shop as we're crossing the street, making me wonder what we're getting ourselves into.

I glance at Ally. "You sure about this?"

"We have to try."

She leads me to the doors, and we push through slowly.

Inside is crawling with shades. They drift through the aisles, baskets in hand, just like regular shoppers only all the life's been sucked out of them.

With Ally's talisman between us we're invisible to them, but I watch the freaks closely under flickering fluorescent lights. Some are tight-lipped, others' mouths gape and drool, showing rotting teeth. They carry their baskets like dead weight, and what's in them is all wrong — rotten fruit, half empty bags of chips and dented cans. The air in here is cold with so many around.

Ally guides me down an aisle silently, using her free hand to pocket a packet of two-minute noodles along the way.

"Backroom," she whispers, and we reach the end of the shelves to watch the all-black plant its bug.

A line of twine stretches across a set of double doors, dangling feathers, shells and dented cans. The shade walks straight to it and stops, twitches up, and puts its card among a pile of bugs beneath it. I can see torn receipts, coins and a few other fake cards.

Ally raises her hand in a signal for us to wait.

But it's no good. The place is full of shades, milling about the shop, drawn in by the stack of bugs at the backroom door. As soon as one leaves this end of the shop another shows up.

I wonder how long before they start shopping for us?

I squeeze Ally's hand with my sweaty one and whisper, "This is sketchy, we should go."

Her eyes lock onto mine with a fire behind them that tells me there's no way we're not trying to save this poor sucker.

My stomach churns. The air cold and full of static with so many of shuffling around like zombies. I want to bail.

Ally pulls me close and whispers in my ear. *"Use your lighter when we bust in. Just spark it and hold it up. I'll do the door."*

I don't like it, but I'm not going to tell her that again. She watches a shade shuffle past and holds three fingers up, then two, then one.

I take a deep breath.

Ally pulls me on while I spark Fred's lighter and the nearby shades twitch up and look away.

I hear her bust open the door and turn my head to see that she's kicked the bugs away and is ducking under the string boundary line.

Ally pulls me under while I'm still holding the flame up, and we get through the doors.

She closes them while I release the button on the BIC and gulp in musky air.

It's dark, but warmer in here. Ally flicks on her torch while I shake my scorched thumb.

There's shuffling behind the shelves and Ally whispers, *"Hello?"*

I hear breathing and a sniffle.

"Hello?" she says, louder this time.

A girl jumps out at us from behind the shelves.

She's younger than us, looks terrified, with wide eyes and trembling hands. One holds a cracked watch up, warding us off like we're a pair of shades. The other holds a kitchen knife, shaking in the space between us and reflecting the light off Ally's torch.

Ally puts a hand out. "It's okay we're here to help you."

The girl is twitchy as hell, confused and afraid by the sight of us and looking to the closed door where we came.

I pull Ally back. "Shades, Ally."

Her face drops, then she realises what I mean. I take the sunglasses off my face and so does she.

This makes the girl put her watch away, which would be a relief if she didn't grip the knife with two hands instead now.

I wish she would but Ally doesn't back away.

"We came cause we saw a shade carrying a bugged card. I'm Ally and this is Jack. You can't stay here. They know you're in here and they're coming."

The girl just grits her teeth and says nothing, eyes twitching from one of us to the other.

"She thinks we're renegades Ally."

BANG, BANG, BANG

"Police. Open the door."

FIVE

Ally turns to me with her green eyes wide. She looks more afraid than I've ever seen her.

I can't think of anything better to do than yank on the shelf by the door.

Boxes and cans go crashing down and the shelf smashes into the floor.

When I turn I see Ally dart towards the loading bay but the girl steps in front of her, waving the knife in the air.

"Not so fast," she says with a voice no longer trembling.

"Your talismans. Give 'em."

Ally shakes her head.

BANG, BANG, BANG

"Police. Open the door."

I start to say something but my words catch.

"Ally —"

She's pulled out Cass's knife.

"Leave. Now."

The renegade girl opens the roller door and my stomach drops.

Two blokes and a mean-looking chick stand on the pavement holding cricket bats and knives.

The renegade girl smiles at Ally.

"Talismans, tethers, all your shit. On the floor."

Another pounding rattles the door.

That's when I have a wild idea.

"Ally! On me!"

She turns, looking at me confused as I back away into the corner.

She doesn't know what I'm thinking but she trusts me and leaps over.

I rip on the shelf blocking the door as hard as I can and wrap one arm around Ally, the other reaching for Fred's lighter.

We push back into the corner as police bust through — hats, sunnies, gloves and all.

I spark up the lighter and my breath goes still in my throat.

The renegades who were gawking at us split and the shades follow them down the street.

More of them filter through from the shop, through the backroom and out the loading bay, driven out by the lighter like smoke.

Ally entwines her talisman's ribbon through my fingers and she gives them a squeeze with affectionate strength.

I can hardly hold my breath any longer so I let the flame on the lighter die and the room plunges into darkness.

Ally's lips find mine and she kisses me hard.

It feels unreal with all the adrenaline, and we stay locked together in the darkness for seconds.

The shades have all shuffled out and we pull apart, walking hand in hand back through the shop.

There's far less of them in here now and Ally leads me along silently. She pockets a KitKat on the way out and winks at me.

We hit the street and both immediately look around, worried about the renegades, but they're nowhere to be seen.

Ally turns to me.

"We can't trust *anyone*."

"You're telling me."

"At least we got some noodles out of it."

"You were scary — *Leave. Now.*"

She swipes her red hair from her face. "You were smart. That thing with the door and the lighter — I had no idea what you were about to do."

I smile. She trusted me with her life.

Ally embraces me again and I lead her down the main road of South Hobart.

* * * * *

After that whole ordeal we skip scavenging and go straight home.

71

As we step inside the smell of Ally washes over me and I immediately feel comfortable. She puts the heater on while I collapse onto a fluffy cushioned seat.

I take my shoes off with the pure joy of someone who's been on their feet most of the day, and Ally does the same, kicking off her blunnies and dropping onto a seat of her own.

"Some day," she says.

"Only one card after all that."

I watch as Ally's expression goes from exhausted to sly.

She pulls a tarot card out of her pocket and holds it up for me to see.

'*The Renegades.*'

It's white paint pen on black. Three figures standing round holding various weapons, just like what we saw today.

I grin back at Ally. "Where'd you get that?"

"Behind the KitKat." She looks to the card. "Do you want this now? The memories can be a lot."

I nod. "It's fine. Better to get it over with."

Ally passes the tarot card.

Everything goes whack as memories flood my mind. None of it's good. I remember school bullies, confrontations, enemies and times I've had the shit beaten out of me.

After a second, I can let go and Ally takes the card, putting it with the others by her cracked teapot shrine.

"What did you remember?"

"Just shitty stuff."

Ally hugs me and says, "I remember from watching Cass — not all cards bring good memories. One made her cry for a whole day."

"Things to look forward to. Do you mind me asking what card?"

Ally blinks, pulls the knife out of her pocket and flashes the side of the handle with the wolf on it.

"The card was *The Dog*.'"

"Ah yeah," I say, and stop myself from prying further.

"For what it's worth," replies Ally, standing up and stretching. Her shoulders ease back and she shakes out the tension from the day. "I think you're pretty damn useful. And look what I got from the IGA," she says, pulling out the KitKat. "It's not a bad memory, it's a very tasty one."

She makes me smile. After everything, Ally's still found a way to win.

I pull on her hand and she falls into my lap.

"You're a very tasty one — mind sharing?"

Ally grins. She puts a hand to her mouth and makes her eyes go wide playfully.

"Me?" she whispers in shock, then points to the KitKat as if it's some holy artefact. *"Or?"*

I laugh, swipe the KitKat, and kiss her hard.

Eventually Ally pulls away.

"We have noodles," she says, slapping her pocket which makes a satisfying plastic sound.

"The spoils of war, aye."

"Come on," she says, getting up. "Didn't you say you were starving?"

I was starving, only that kiss has got me feeling a different kind of hunger.

We go to the cramped kitchen. Ally moves slowly and gracefully. Here in her home her fire is tempered — it's warm and soft, no longer so desperate.

"That girl," she says, taking the chicken flavoured sachets out of the packets. "That renegade, she almost had us."

"They would've taken everything. Our tethers. We could have died."

"And the thing is they know exactly what they're asking for. They think if they get enough talismans and tethers they'll be untouchable but it's not like that."

"What's it like?"

Ally drains the noodles with a fork. "They think strength comes from what they take. They see our talismans, our tethers, our memories, and they think they're prizes to be stolen." She points her fork at me, a fleck of noodle on the end of it. "But it's not about stealing, Jack. It's about sharing. It's about finding people and not being alone in this."

I watch as she cracks the sachets and stirs the flavour through.

"So… where does strength come from?"

Ally sets a steaming bowl of noodles in front of me and rolls her eyes.

"Sharing, not stealing."

For a while it's just us eating dinner to the sound of the heater. We are quiet and comfortable together. Each thinking our own thoughts.

When I get up afterwards I go over to Ally's shrine.

I'm picking through the cards, savouring the memories, when one falls out of the pile I've never seen before.

'*The Bucks*' shows a picture of me and Fred sitting side by side playing tunes at the pub. We look well past merry and are both grinning like idiots.

The moment I pick it up I'm happier than I've been since I got here. My favourite tunes surge in my ears, the sound of me on the fiddle and Fred on the guitar playing *The Bucks of Oranmore* and *The Boys of Malin*. The whole pub going into uproar as we race into a big finish.

"It's a bug," says Ally, but I don't hear her.

Not until she is standing right beside me.

"It's a bug."

With a deft hand Ally snatches the card from my fingers, then stares at me poignantly.

The memory shatters and my mood snaps like someone shit in my lunchbox.

I turn to Ally and she's shaking her head.

"Isn't that fucked up? One crossed the boundary line when we weren't here and planted this. Use your lighter, Jack. Destroy it."

"I was remembering. It's a real card."

Silence stretches and I realise I yelled.

Ally just stares at me.

"It's a bug, Jack. A bad one. It's trying to trick you."

"It's not. It feels just like the others. Only this one — *it's Fred, Ally* — *he was so happy.*"

Before I know it I've snatched the card back off Ally and the memories make my eyes swim.

Fred grins at me, head banging, foot stamping, hand pounding the guitar.

"Dickhead!" yells Ally, and the reminiscence is derailed entirely.

There standing beside me is the Empress of Fire and she is pissed.

I think I'm about to be slapped in the face, but she just stares at me. I don't know what's worse.

Ally's fists are clenched and her chest is puffed up. The fire in her eyes burns molten hot. She lets out a long shuddery breath and her gaze drops to the card in my hand.

"Don't you get it, Jack?" her voice now dangerously calm. "You're holding onto a lie. That card isn't bringing you closer to Fred. That card is a bug and it'll take control of you if you let it."

The warmth of the card is muted by the bitter cold of her words.

Why is she so against Fred?

For a moment I feel the card for what it is. A whispering bug. A lie.

The image of Fred flickers, then it pulls me in even harder than before and Ally's words cut me deep.

I hesitate, but then the words come out of my mouth.

"You're jealous."

Ally's mouth flies open. *"Jealous?!"*

"You're jealous of me and Fred. Jealous of my memories!"

"You really think so?"

I nod and clutch the card to my chest. Ally is livid. She points with a shaky finger to the card.

"It's the bug, Jack. It's making you act like this."

"No Ally, it's you."

I can see her eyes water, and I know my words hurt her.

"Get fucked!"

She tries to snatch the card away from me.

This time I'm ready, and I pull away, fending her off so she can't get the card.

But it's messy — I accidentally shove her back too hard, into one of her paintings.

The canvas comes crashing down and catches on the coffee table, ripping a massive hole in the picture.

Right through the bit that says, *"How do I get out of my labyrinth of fire?"*

Ally freezes.

My heart stops.

"Out."

"Get the fuck out."

The image of her standing there like that gets burnt into my mind permanently.

By now I know that I fucked up, but it's too late. There's nothing for it but to leave.

"I'm sorry Ally."

She just shakes her head and sighs, pointing to the door.

I pick up my tarot cards and go.

As I reach the door I hear her sniffle, and when I look back she's got her head in her hands. I think she's crying, but she's facing the other way so I can't tell.

I feel sick.

I want to turn around and beg her forgiveness, but some part of me wants to leave just to spite her.

I swing the creaky door open, slam it behind me, and step out into the dusk, the huge trees in the street crawling with shadows.

SIX

I wander aimlessly clutching my tarot cards. Ally's words echo in my head, and so does the image of her standing there so pissed off she was visibly shaking.

My thoughts are a mess, but Fred is there guiding me. I can almost hear his voice.

"You did the right thing man. Forget about her, the universe will sort you out."

The memories of him set me at ease, but it's getting dark, and I have nowhere to go.

A nearby shade I pass seems to pause and turn its head, sunglasses locking onto me for a second.

I reach for the lighter talisman around my neck, but I don't have to use it.

Now that I'm paying attention, I notice that every shade I pass seems to notice me to some degree.

It's off-putting as hell — without Ally's talisman I'm exposed.

I clutch my tarot cards tight, and the feel of them comforts me. Without Ally to distract me I'll be able to find them all.

I need to get to a shrine, and I run through my options.

I could go back to Ally but that's not happening.

I could go to her shrine at Cascade Gardens but that's hers.

I could try fix the one in the backroom of the IGA but the renegades might show up.

It leaves me with one choice — repair the shrine at the New Sydney Hotel.

* * * * *

Bathurst Street is all wrong. Hardly a car goes past as I'm walking down, and they go slowly, with broken lights, wonky mirrors and lifeless drivers behind the wheel wearing sunglasses even though it's dark now.

The Tassie night air is cold and the breeze bites. I powerwalk with my arms at my chest to keep warm, my stack of tarot cards tight in hand.

They give me the will to carry on. The promise of getting out of this nightmare. The promise of returning to Fred so we can play music and laugh again, like the good old times.

As I'm approaching the New Syd a shade out the front tilts her head at me. I almost laugh because she looks so bizarre. Instead of black sunglasses she has these massive pink ones, and she's standing there with her weight on one leg, smoking a cigarette but at the wrong end.

I move past briskly and try not to worry about the fact she seemed to notice me. Maybe she's a different type of shade. One that's more powerful.

Ally would probably know.

The thought of her stings but thankfully I have no time to dwell there. I just turn the handle of the front door and step inside.

The pub is completely different to when I was here last.

The shrine that was bugged is still there on the bar, and the place is still packed with shades, but there's warmth, and music — real music — not the distorted stuff with static in it that was playing last time.

There's a lively session with fiddles and flutes, mandolins, guitars and drums, all played by musicians with unseen eyes. I recognise the tune — *Julia Delaney's Reel*.

One of the shades sees me standing there gawking and offers up his fiddle.

I'm ecstatic. I'm going to play one for Fred — *The Bucks of Oranmore* — his favourite tune.

Not a moment after I've sat down and taken the fiddle, a shade is there standing beside me with a pint of Guinness in hand. It's the bar staff. An all-black.

I grab the Guinness and smile at him, take a sip, then nearly choke.

I'm coughing my guts up, spitting Guinness everywhere, then I look in the glass and see a few dead flies swirling around in the foam.

"No flames in the bar, mate. I'll take that."

My stomach drops as I turn to see the shade with his arm outstretched, grinning with rotten teeth.

That's when I realise Ally was right.

The music stops. The lights flicker. When they come back every shade sitting in the session has set their instruments down. They're all facing me, staring with eyes I can't see.

Fuck.

Thank fuck for Ally.

I manage to spark the lighter before the shade next to me can get it, only because it's been made into a necklace, no — a talisman, by the Empress of Fire.

The shades closest to me twitch and thrash as I take to my feet with the flame burning.

The static in my ears is so loud I might as well be standing in the middle of a thunderstorm for all else I could hear.

I bolt out the door, frightened for my life.

Not looking look back, I just run up the street flicking through my tarot cards, finding the bugged card and ripping it into pieces. They trail through the air after me falling one by one.

I've been running without thinking, and only now realise I'm headed straight for Ally's house which is a big no.

If I get there it'll be bugged to shit and I'll have ruined her one safe place.

Instead, I take the next right and head straight for the bottom of the rivulet track.

The shrine at Cascade Gardens will give me what I need to lose them, even if it gets bugged in the process. Then I can get back to Ally.

If she'll still have me.

But when I look back my hopes sink.

There must be twenty shades following behind me. And those are just the ones I can see.

When I jog they jog.

When I run they run.

Whatever pace I pick up, they match it, not twenty metres behind me.

The sound of their shoes against the gravel is all wrong.

There's static, bits of sound missing, and it mingles into the sounds of them whispering satanically.

I hear fragments of bad memories.

Mum's voice.

"You can go live with your father if you want to be a deadshit."

Fred's voice.

"You don't cut yourself out of the deck Jack. This is serious shit man."

Worst of all are the whispers in Ally's voice. They actually make me cry.

"Get the fuck out."

"Get the fuck out," over and over again.

I was so wrong.

She was so right.

The bug twisted me. And it nearly cost me everything straight away.

The boundary line at Cascade is such a relief.

I cross over and my guts fall out when I see the mob of shades reach the cairn stones.

They drop bug after bug. Fake cards, pieces of musical instruments, shards of pint glasses, I even see one drop a dead fly into the cairn stones.

I scramble to remove them but they come faster than I can take them away, and all of a sudden I'm lost in what is a charm and what is a bug.

Ally.

I need Ally.

A shade reaches over the boundary line and I pull my hand away, jumping back like I've just seen a massive spider.

The boundary line is bugged to all hell.

The shrine is useless.

I sprint across the grass between the huge pine trees towards it, nearly slipping on the wet grass. With static in my ears, the park benches come into view and I see Ally standing beside the shrine.

"The boundary is fucked, Ally!

"I saw them you dickhead! And you came here!"

As I'm running up to her she pulls out a Gatorade bottle and pours it all over one of the park benches.

I turn my head to see shades following behind me, but whip it back around when Ally says, *"Lighter! Now!"*

In the panic I have no idea what she's doing but I trust her.

As I'm running, I take off the necklace Ally made with the broken fiddle string, Fred's lighter and feathers.

I pass it to Ally as soon as she's in reach.

She lights the park bench on fire.

Whatever she poured on it goes up like petrol.

Ally and I stand beside two park benches. One is on fire, the other has the beautiful shrine she made on it. All around us are shades of various types.

They all twitch up and walk away. The whole horde of them. They don't even drop bugs or anything.

"We have to move the shrine Jack."

I turn to Ally and she is more beautiful than ever in the light of the bonfire.

Her body is saturated in heat and her messy red hair blows all around her in the wind. The light of the fire fills her big eyes.

"I'm sorry Ally."

She pulls me into her, and we're locked together in the heat of the fire. The smell of burning varnish mixes with the cold night air.

"It's okay. It was the card."

"I'm so sorry."

Ally pulls apart from me, but holds my shoulders.

"It's okay. But Jack. You have to know. I have my match but you started with it. It's a tether, yeah. But my real tether is you, Jack."

Then she says it.

"I love you."

"I—."

Ally collides into me in the light of the bonfire. We lose ourselves.

Static in the air

The shades are closing in

Petrol, a spark, a hope and a hunch

Up in flames, goes the spot for lunch

Ashes in the air

Eyes of pyre

Is this the way out

Of my labyrinth of fire?

SEVEN

Ally and I break apart.

"That won't last long," she says, with flames dancing in her eyes.

"Did you say we have to move the shrine?"

"Mmm."

Ally dismantles it while I hold open her bag and collect the charms and Carl Jung book.

We're silent while we work together. There are a million things I want to say to her, but now isn't the time.

After the bag is zipped up, Ally hangs my talisman back around my neck, kisses me on the nose, then offers her hand with the braided ribbons of her talisman in it.

We leave Cascade Gardens as the fire is burning lower, and Ally pockets some of the charms from the boundary line along the way.

"They'll still be after us," she says. "We need to set up this shrine before going home or they'll do the same thing there."

"But where do we set up?" I ask as we walk out onto the carpark.

Ally grins at me.

"I say we get ourselves a car."

After everything that's happened I can't help but laugh a little, half at the words, half at the look on her face.

"What's so funny. Don't you know how to drive?"

"No idea. Do you?"

"Actually, I can't remember either. You'd think one of us can, wouldn't you?"

I laugh again. "There's one way to find out. But whose car are we stealing?"

Ally smiles and points to a white Toyota Corolla that must be about thirty years old. It's beat up, riddled with dents, with flaky paint, and one headlight is completely smashed.

"You got keys?"

Ally pulls a flathead screwdriver out of her bag.

"This is our key."

She sticks it in the door and I know it's going to open because I can see a tarot card on the dash.

Click.

She turns and grins at me. "Who's driving?"

"You can. I think I can drive, but you have the first turn — you earnt it."

Ally jumps in and I take to the passenger.

"Well we've got plenty of fuel. Just let me try this for a sec."

Ally slides the flathead into the ignition, jiggles it around a bit, then turns her wrist.

The car starts with a beautiful decrepit hum.

She turns to me with an electric look on her face. "Fuck yes!"

We shove the seats back and she opens her bag over the top of the handbrake.

First comes out the Carl Jung book with braided ribbons wrapped all around it like a spider's web. Ally fiddles with it for a second with her clever fingers, then hangs the book from the mirror.

Together we attach charms, threading them into the ribbons. Soon feathers and leaves and shells all dangle from the book, and the central shrine is complete.

"Good," says Ally. "Charm up the outside and we've got a mobile boundary line. Hey! Isn't that one of your cards."

I eye it off as it sits on the dash.

"The Chariot of Fire" depicts a car just like the one we are sitting in. White paint pen makes sharp lines all around it to show movement.

"Let's just wait till we're rolling."

"You're right. It looks like a happy one though."

I take a few more charms out the bag and so does Ally. Together we get out of the car and plaster on as many as we can using masking tape from her painting studio.

It looks ridiculous with all the trinkets, but Ally's happier than I've ever seen her. She adds the finishing touch — torn prayer flags tied to the towbar, and we get back in.

Ally changes into reverse and we back out sharply, her foot a little heavy on the pedal. I don't think she can drive but luckily it's an auto and the streets are dead.

"Ready?"

I lean over and plant a kiss on her cheek.

"Ready."

We swing up and out of the Cascade Gardens and turn left onto the main road of South Hobart.

I pick the tarot card off the dash and memories flood back to me.

I had a car just like this. Fred and I used to drive around smoking with the windows down, blasting tunes. It was my first and only car.

I wind the window down and cold air rushes in.

It's perfect. I'm euphoric.

I turn to Ally and the sight of her hunched over the wheel is beyond beautiful.

She is grinning from ear to ear, and with one hand she winds down her window and the wind blows her hair everywhere.

"Woohooooo!" she yells, and I do the same.

"Good memories?!"

"The best!"

"I've never driven before!"

"I know! You're doing great though!"

"Where do you wanna go?!"

"Over the bridge!"

"Fuck yes!"

I go through the glovebox and find it's my lucky day. Inside is a pack of Winfield Blues.

I spark one up with Fred's lighter.

"You want one?!" I yell to Ally, over the sound of the road.

"I don't smoke but fuck it, I'll have one."

I spark Ally's dart and together we are ecstatic, cruising down into the city and hardly stopping for red lights.

"You came back for me!"

"Of course I did you dickhead!"

"How did you know where to find me?!"

"I had a hunch! I knew you'd probably go to Cascade so I cut down onto the rivulet by the school! I saw the mob after you so I ran ahead!"

"The fire! — the park bench!"

Ally turns and grins. "A girl's gotta have a few tricks up her sleeve!"

"Or a bottle of petrol in her handbag!"

"Was a total hunch that it would work because of your tether! And I am the Empress of Fire after all!"

"You are! Oh Empress! I can see the Tasman Bridge!"

The lights on the bridge flicker, and only a scattering of headlights cross it, but all of it is reflected on the black Derwent and the moon hangs full over the Eastern shore.

I hold my cigarette out the window for a second and the ashes go flying, then I flick on the radio, finding the volume knob in the dark and cranking it.

Static erupts from the speakers and I wince as the energy in the car shatters.

It's the sound of shades, and I kill it right away.

"Well I guess there's no radio."

Ally laughs. "No matter."

"ON THE ROAD AGAIN!"

"I JUST CAN'T WAIT TO GET BACK ON THE ROAD AGAIN!"

I laugh and join in yelling the lyrics completely out of key.

We hit the bridge.

Ally's driving.

I'm flying.

I'm happier than I've been since I landed in this fucked up version of Hobart. Maybe even happier than I was before I got here.

For a moment I'm sad listening to Ally sing so badly and happily.

I wonder if I find all my cards — will I really be able to save her?

And what happens when I wake up? — it seems childish to think that she'll just be there, and she'll wake up too.

I shake my head.

Enjoy the moment, Jack.

* * * * *

Ally pulls her top back on, the cotton sticking with sweat. We get out of the backseat and stand watching the view.

From the Rosny Hill lookout the city twinkles with a thousand lights reflecting on the river, and Kunanyi looms like the sprawling body of a great sleeping dragon.

I light a dart using Fred's red BIC and I am high on life.

Ally is right by my side. I know deep down that nothing will ever be better than this.

"Don't ever leave me again," she says.

"Never."

EIGHT

The sun is warm on my face as we walk along the shoreline of Roches beach. We left the city behind. The salt air makes a haze where it catches the light. It's clean and refreshing, a welcome change from the static of the city and the constant threat of shades.

Ally and I have been on the road for a few days. We've fallen into a rhythm — spending the mornings scavenging for charms, food and water, then card hunting in the afternoons.

Together we've found three more already and the memories restored led us here, to my childhood beach.

Ally bends over a patch of wet sand and picks up a triangular shaped rock.

"Look!" she says. "It's Tassie!"

I laugh. "Vaguely." Then I spot a good piece of blue seaglass and pick it up.

"How bout this one Empress?"

Ally smiles, taking it from my hand and brushing the sand off. "It's perfect," she says, and tucks it into her bag with the other trinkets.

We spend a quiet hour like this, our conversation in peaceful fragments.

I like Ally at the beach, she's calm and her hair goes everywhere — the way I like it. For the first time since I arrived here, I've almost forgotten about the shades, and our time together feels like a real date. A perfect moment in time.

The car is parked at the Yacht Club, and we soon head back.

I'm walking up the boat ramp when I see it.

The Mitsubishi Lancer from my first day here. It's charmed-up even more, with wallaby skulls and multiple pairs of cracked sunglasses dangling out the boot, parked behind our car to block it from reversing.

My heart sinks.

Ally and I stop as she sees it too.

That's when he comes out of the bushes holding a rifle.

The renegade is tall — late twenties — a fully grown man dressed in combat boots, camo pants and a black CAT jacket.

His eyes go wide as he points the rifle at us and yells.

"The lighter! Drop it and leave!"

I freeze up and look to Ally. She's standing with her feet apart, ready to fight, Cass's knife with the wolf decal in her hand.

"I'll shoot her! Try anything mate and I'll shoot her fair in the chest!"

We are trapped.

I reach for my neck and my fingers close around Fred's lighter. My one tether to the real world — the only talisman I've ever had, and it was made by Ally herself.

But the look in the man's eyes is wild and manic. I know he's not bluffing. This isn't a game.

"Like hell you will!" yells Ally.

"She's fiery, mate. Shame to waste her. Now I'm only after the lighter. You can keep the girl. You can keep the car too. It's your lucky day as far as I'm concerned."

My heart pounds in my chest. There's no choice here. I won't risk Ally's life, not even for mine. This isn't a negotiation — it's an ambush.

I quickly pull the necklace over my head.

"Jack! What are you doing?!"

For a second I try think of something I could do — some trick with the lighter. But the renegade is a real person, not a shade. I toss it through the air and the bastard catches it perfectly.

For a moment the gun isn't pointed at Ally and she steps forward.

I pull her back

"Good boy," says the renegade, and I'm seething.

He smiles. "I'm going to burn so many freaks with this. Piss off now."

CRACK

He fires a shot into the gravel at our feet, making us jump.

I take Ally by the hand and lead her back down to the beach.

"What the fuck?"

I throw up my hands. "What was I supposed to do? Let him shoot you?"

Ally shakes her head and goes quiet.

I turn and watch as the Lancer drives away, kicking up dust from the gravel.

"I'm sorry Ally."

I watch as my words soften her. She wriggles the tension out of her shoulders and sighs, looking out across the water.

"I'm getting your talisman back."

"How?"

"We find where that cunt lives and do a little ambush of our own."

I just nod, defeated.

"This is serious Jack. If he lets that lighter run at the wrong time... You won't be able to breathe. If it runs out of gas... Jack if you die, I never go home. I might as well be shot."

I look out to the sea in silence.

"How do we do it?"

"I've seen that Lancer before. I've seen it parked in Salamanca twice."

"You reckon he has a shrine there?"

"I'd bet on it."

"What's the plan th—"

I can't breathe. The renegade is using my talisman.

My chest locks. I'm drowning in sunlight and choking on nothing.

Ally's mouth opens wide, realising what's happening. She sees the panic in my eyes and hugs me tight.

"Fuck Jack. This is not okay."

After a couple seconds I can breathe again, and Ally pulls back but still holds onto my hands.

"*Scary.* Are you okay?"

I nod.

"Let's go to Salamanca."

Ally nods back at me. "We go to Salamanca and find this shrine. We can work out a plan to get your talisman back from there. Oh, and you're not driving until we get it."

I love Ally's confidence. It makes me feel better.

I just hope this works out.

* * * * *

Ally pulls the car around the corner from Irish Murphys. She drives it up in the very back corner of a massive carpark so that it's out of sight and kills the engine.

We turn to each other.

"Let's do this," she says.

"Where do we start?"

"Doesn't matter. We go through the whole of Salamanca. We know he hasn't set up at Murphy's so we don't bother checking there. We are close to the Whaler though. We should look there for starters."

We get out of the car and Ally locks it with her screwdriver key, then offers up her talisman-entwined hand.

Together we set off down the street. I feel naked without my own talisman, but I know I'm safe so long as I hold onto Ally's hand.

The shades in the street ignore us, and we don't see any sign of the Lancer on the way down to the Whaler.

Out the front of the pub there's plenty of shades. Together we drift past them and poke our heads inside.

But the pub is all wrong.

A band wearing sunglasses plays distorted metal by the door and static fills my ears as I look around and see the place just as I expected it — crawling with shades. No sign of a shrine.

Ally looks to me and I don't have to say anything, we just leave.

Out around the corner my breath catches again and Ally's concerned.

She reaches out to hold my cheek with one hand and the moment passes.

I need that lighter.

Ally whispers so the shades can't hear. *"Well, the Whaler's a bust. I say we hit Preachers since it's just up the road."*

By now I'm feeling pretty hopeless about the whole thing, but I don't tell her that.

I just nod and walk along with her up the hill.

Soon we round the corner, onto the small side street where Preachers is.

We look over the ivy-choked fence and there are no shades here. From where I am the pub looks deserted.

I don't get my hopes up. There are no charms hanging from the fence. But then I see the bus — that cooky bus that lives in the beer garden, and I am overjoyed.

I stop and point at all the dangling charms I can see through the windows and Ally's face lights up.

She makes a 'shh' gesture with her free hand and we slink up the footpath to the front step.

I'm looking around but I don't see anyone. I don't think he's here but we still go quietly and slowly, prowling through the deserted beer garden and up to the bus.

The doors are wide open, so we go straight in.

The entire bus has been decked out with charms, and at the end of the aisle I see the shrine — a collection of charms on the backseat surrounding the central item — a stolen sign that's dented to shit and reads: *'Designated Smoking Area.'*

"What now?"

Ally shrugs her shoulders. "He's not here."

"But he could be any second. *With a gun.*"

"We fuck up this shrine. Wait outside for him to get here. He goes inside. We bust into his car and get the lighter." Ally grins. "Oh and I say we fuck his car over too. I've refilled my Gatorade bottle."

I grin back at her. "We need bugs, Ally — The New Syd? Cascade?"

She nods, "You're right. This'll work better if we bug it. The New Sydney is a quick in and out. You drive, pull up out the very front while I go in with my talisman. I'll shove the whole bugged shrine into my bag and we get the fuck out."

* * * * *

We do exactly as we discussed.

I pull up by the front door to the pub and Ally jumps out. Here in the car with the shrine I'm safe without her talisman.

But I'm nervous for her.

Thankfully Ally is quick as a whip and runs back out before I have time to freak out.

She hurls the bag into the car and jumps in. We drive off while shades swarm out through the door and onto the footpath.

Ally sighs.

"Nicely done."

"Why thank you."

I drive fast with all the bugs in the car, worried we might pass some cops or something. But it's a safe trip all the way back to Salamanca.

Instead of using the car park around the corner, I pull up out the front of Preachers and Ally runs out with her bag.

She quickly returns, carrying the bent sign from the shrine, and jumping back in the car. I start driving immediately, headed for the carpark we used earlier.

"I fucked the shrine, found a bunch of supplies too. I'm guessing this renegade has a few shrines going — places to fall back on when the others get compromised."

"Makes sense. It's smart really. We should do the same."

Ally nods, "Yeah," then shakes out her body like she's trying to get rid of a shiver.

"Ugh! Those bugs! That was a lot."

"You're okay now though," I reply.

Turning into the carpark, Ally trembles.

"Cass's voice. It's always Cass's voice. I could hear her screaming so loud in my ears. The same screams as when she got taken by the Faceless."

I don't know what to say. Grief like that feels so alien to me. I just rest a hand on Ally's thigh. Her hand finds mine and I give it a strong squeeze.

"Okay," I say as I use the flathead to kill the engine.

"Let's do this."

NINE

We've been waiting in the bushes just up the street from Preachers for a few hours when the renegade finally shows up.

I had lost hope, but here he is, parking his charmed-up Lancer out the front of the beer garden and getting out with my talisman around his neck.

Bastard.

Ally squeezes my hand. "This is it, Jack. As soon as he hits the gate we go."

We watch the renegade bastard looking around confused. He sees the shades milling about the bar and must be wondering what happened to his shrine. He goes to the gate.

Good boy.

"He's got the lighter," whispers Ally, as we take to the street and crouch-run to the car treading as softly as we can.

It's locked, but Ally tries it with her flathead screwdriver and manages to open the door.

THE EMPRESS OF FIRE

I look in and the car is messy, with a small shrine in the centre console formed around a singed Marlboro packet which Ally swipes.

There on the back seat is the rifle that bastard pointed at us.

Ally goes for it straight away and pulls the gun through the open door.

Not a moment after, the renegade is there at the top of the street with my talisman around his neck.

"Oi! The fuck do you think you're doing?!"

Ally turns, aims the rifle, and the renegade stops dead in his tracks. A few shades have noticed by now, and they're starting to creep out of the beer garden.

"The lighter! Give us our fucking lighter back before I put a bullet in your head."

The renegade clenches his jaw, looks around, sees the shades staring, then slowly he takes the necklace off and throws it to me.

I just manage to catch it, and Ally whispers, *"Do you think he wants some Gatorade in his car or what? — in my bag."*

I dig it out of Ally's bag while she distracts him.

"What's your name you renegade bastard?"

"Riley."

"Well you really fucked it this time Riley."

I find the bottle, twist the cap off and spray it in the inside of the car, chucking the half-empty thing at the shrine in the console.

I light up the car and it goes with a *whoosh*.

"Get fucked," says Riley, his eyes narrowed. *"You're going to regret that."*

Ally grits her teeth. "Fuck with us again and I'll put a bullet in you!"

I place a hand on Ally's shoulder and guide her back down the footpath while she holds the gun aimed at Riley.

He splits off in the other direction with shades behind him.

Ally and I go around the corner and out of sight.

From there we sprint back to the carpark.

With all the adrenaline surging through my body and my talisman swinging from my neck as I run, I feel euphoric.

"You were fucking awesome Ally!"

"We did it together," she says, passing me the flathead.

This time I'm driving and I crank the engine as fast as I can.

Ally slides the rifle onto the backseat. She reaches over and runs her fingers through my hair.

"Let's get the fuck out of here."

* * * * *

I drive us across the bridge, putting as much distance between us and Riley as possible. We can't let him know where we live.

After all that we need a breather, so I take the turnoff up to the Rosny Hill lookout. There we sit in the car and talk.

"We need to make a backup shrine."

Ally nods. "This side of the river. What if our car breaks down."

"Any ideas?"

"Somewhere where there's already food."

"Salamanca Fresh? In Bellerive?"

"Worth checking out."

Ally is silent.

"Are you okay Ally?"

She shakes her head. "Not really. I'm pretty shaken up."

I put a hand on her. "That was pretty hectic."

"Yeah. As far as I know I've never pointed a gun at someone before."

"You did great Ally. It's over now."

She frowns. "Is it Jack? Part of me thinks I should have shot him. He's going to come back after us. Of course he is."

"We'll be ready. We have his gun. We have this car. We'll make a backup shrine. We'll be okay."

"How much of your lighter did he use?"

I shake the thing — it's still got a bit of juice in it. The number on the barcode reads: ...001897

"There's a bit less than half of what I started with left."

Ally looks to me, more serious than ever. "You can't waste it anymore Jack. Find something else to light your darts with. When that lighter runs out you die and I might as well be dead too."

She turns my hand over in hers.

"If you go there's nothing left for me here. If you go I'm letting them take me."

"You can't Ally. You have to keep going. There has to be another way out for you."

"There wasn't — and then there was — my only way out is you, Jack. We have to find those cards. Find all of them before something terrible happens. How many do you have now?"

I'm not sure so I take the stack of tarot cards out of the glove box and count them.

"Twelve and a half. Hey, where do you reckon the other half of 'The Card-Cutter' is?"

"No idea, but I have a suspicion it'll be the last one."

"How many cards in a tarot deck?"

"Seventy-eight."

My jaw drops. "Fuck."

"It's not like that though, there's only twenty-two major arcana cards. The rest are the suits."

"So we only need to find ten more?"

Ally nods and I smile at her. She smiles back.

"We're over half-way already."

Now she's grinning.

"You know I quite like the sound of that actually."

I reach for my Winnie Blue and look to Ally, holding the lighter dangling from my neck.

"Last one. I'll find a new sparkler at Sal Fresh."

The look on her face makes me feel guilty but she doesn't tell me what to do, she just puts a hand on my thigh and says, "Sal Fresh eh?"

* * * * *

I pull our Corolla into what used to be the bustling car-park of a popular grocery store. The sign above the door reads: "Salamanca Fresh," in a flaky decal, and the steel apple beside it is rusted and hanging wonky.

We get out. There are a few shades around but with our talismans they completely ignore us.

Around the back of the building we go, straight to the loading bay, and there Ally uses a crowbar on the steel doors.

With a few good, strong pulls, she gets it open and we go inside.

"Gross," says Ally, wrinkling her nose.

The smell of rotten meat and fruit washes over me. The place is dark and cold, and I can hear the static of nearby shades.

"You still want to do this?"

"We can throw out what's bad," replies Ally, flicking on her torch.

We move through the storage room, past broken palettes and empty shelves looking for a good place to build our shrine.

"Back here," I whisper, pointing to small nook with a desk that must be used as an office space in the real world.

But Ally isn't paying attention to me. Her eyes are fixated on something at the back of the room.

I move around the shelves so I can see it too.

Standing facing the wall is a shade, only something is wrong with it. It's all tense, hunched over and not moving one bit.

Ally whispers to me, *"That's weird. I think it's stuck, Jack."*

I'm curious and move closer.

"Be careful."

The shade still doesn't move, even though I'm only a few metres behind it. I can hear its static.

It whispers to me in Fred's voice, *"You cut us out Jack…"*

The words pull at my mind, making me doubt myself, but I resist, clutching my talisman with one hand.

Bloody freak bastards. I'm sick of them.

Fred's lighter feels solid in my hand. I spark it up and hold the flame to the back of the shade's shirt.

"Jack!"

The fucker goes up like Ally poured petrol on him and I jump back.

Deafening static fills my ears. The shade thrashes violently.

Ally is by my side in an instant. We watch the shade burn up like it's made out of paper, disappearing into ash.

"Why did you have to do that?"

"What do you mean?"

"You just killed a shade."

And then I remember. Ally said the Faceless One appeared when Cass stabbed a shade.

Shit.

"The Faceless. Right."

Ally just shakes her head. "We can't stay here. We have to leave right now."

That's when I spot a tarot card on the shelf near where the shade was.

I point and say, "You take it, we don't have time."

Ally grabs the card and we bail out the way we came.

Out in the carpark it's getting darker and we go straight for our Corolla.

There are more shades around than just a second ago. They mill in and out of the shops, faster than before, and seemingly on edge.

Ally drives, I light a cigarette with Fred's lighter, which warrants a disappointed look from my Empress, but she doesn't say anything.

I can tell she's worried.

"How long did it take for the Faceless to show up?"

"A couple hours."

"Do you think it'll follow us if we go home?"

"Yes."

"Are you pissed at me?"

Ally turns to me with that look on her face — the one that's a mix of frustration and sadness. I hate to see it and feel guilty as hell.

"I'm not pissed at you, Jack. I'm just stressed. What are we going to do? If we go home the Faceless will show up eventually and it'll walk straight through the boundary line."

"Then we leave. We've got this car and we stole heaps of petrol. We should drive somewhere far away until the Faceless forgets about us."

"I don't know if that'll work, but I can't think of anything better to do. Where do you say we go?"

I think for a second, and the idea pops into my head out of nowhere.

"Cygnet. I have a good feeling about Cygnet."

Ally nods and we hit the bridge. "Cygnet it is then. Do you want your card now?"

"Yeah, what was it?"

"See for yourself. I didn't look."

Memories slap me in the face as I stare down at *The Fighter*' card.

For a moment I'm reliving a scrap from college. Fred and I versus four skater kids. Somehow, we won.

It's not a good or bad memory, but it makes me remember who I am.

As soon as I'm able to I put the card in the glovebox with the rest.

I look to Ally and see she's still tense. I wonder if I can get her to relax.

"On the road again…."

TEN

We're flying down the highway, just outside Huonville with Ally at the wheel. It's a good while after dark now, and the air blowing through the window is cold.

I smoke my cigarette.

Ally's gone quiet. I think she's exhausted, and I offer to take the wheel, but she refuses.

"We're not far off. I can manage it."

"You're smashed Ally, let me have a turn."

She sighs, says, "Fine," and pulls over on the side of the road.

We get out to swap seats.

That's when we hear the sound of an engine roaring in the distance.

I turn to face the way we came and see headlights coming towards us.

It's moving fast, faster than any shade car.

"Shit," says Ally. "That's people."

"Renegades?"

"Probably."

"Get the gun Ally. Our car's a shitbox, there's no way we can outrun them."

"You're right."

The car continues to hurtle towards us, but then it slows.

By now Ally is standing with the rifle resting on the boot, and I'm beside her, behind the car.

Now that they're closer we can actually see the car.

It's a charmed-up ute, white, and covered mostly in feathers but other trinkets too. It slows right down, moving at a snail's pace.

Ally aims the rifle at it and I hold the Gatorade bottle at the ready.

Windows wind down and we see some familiar faces.

The ute is packed with the renegades from the IGA in South Hobart, with the girl that tried to trap us sitting on the backseat chewing gum.

One of the blokes does a wolf whistle at Ally and I tense up.

She yells out and stands up tall with the rifle aimed at them.

"Pass by peacefully and I won't shoot! Pass by and you live!"

They just squint at us and for a moment I think they're about to stop and get out but the car keeps rolling along slowly.

I think I hear one of them say, "I want that gun."

I'm ready to douse their car in petrol but it picks up its pace and carries on down the road.

We turn and watch it go.

Ally sighs. "Fucking renegades."

"What now?"

"Same as before. We head to Cygnet and find somewhere to stay. Somewhere we can park the car out of sight. If it's any good we can make a shrine. We have Riley's burnt ciggie packet and the sign from the bus."

"Alright, let's wait a few more minutes and roll out. I'm driving."

* * * * *

We pass through Huonville without incident and no sign of the renegades. Between there and Cygnet it's the same, and I start to relax and my exhaustion from the day catches up on me.

We've just passed Pagan Cider when I pull into a gravel side road.

There's a group of buildings sitting on a few acres and I look to Ally.

She nods.

"This'll have to do."

I park under a birch tree and kill the headlights, then the engine.

We get out quietly and look around with our torches but there are no shades here. I get the feeling no one has been here in a long, long time.

I shine my torch on the buildings. There's a main house, a few sheds and a smaller three-segmented building.

"Which one?" I ask, and Ally points to the latter.

The door is unlocked and inside is full of clutter. It's dead quiet, with not a bit of static in the air. We go to the main room and Ally sets the rifle down on the floor. I do the same with her bag, opening it so we can take out the stuff to build a shrine.

In silence we work together, arranging the charms we've collected over the past few days around Riley's singed Marlboro packet.

Smells a bit like ash but it does the job.

Next we set up the boundary, taping charms to the walls using Ally's masking tape.

"I'm just getting the sleeping bags."

Ally makes a *mwah* sound with her lips and starts doing yoga.

Outside it's freezing and dark so I return quickly and open the sleeping bags up.

I lie down and Ally makes herself comfortable with her head under my arm.

She lets out a long sigh.

"What a day."

"We're safe now."

"For now."

"I know I'm safe as long as I'm with you Ally. You're my shrine."

She smiles and kisses me.

"You're my shrine too. And my tether. Fuck I don't even know if I'd still be here without you."

"Oh you'd still be kicking around."

"I'm not so sure."

"You don't have to think about it," I reply and drop a kiss into her curly red hair.

"What should I think about."

"Don't think about it," I tell her. "Think about me instead."

"Arrogant prick," she says, but smiles into my chest

"I keep thinking about the Faceless."

"It can't get you here."

"It will eventually."

"But we'll keep moving. We'll find a way to stop it. Do you think I can burn it with the lighter?"

"Get close to it and you're gone Jack. I've seen it."

"The gun?"

"I don't know," she replies, and now I can tell she just wants to sleep.

I kiss her forehead. "Goodnight Ally. Love you."

"Love you too."

* * * * *

I wake to Ally sitting upright in our bed. Well it's not much of a bed, just two sleeping bags on a patch of stained carpet.

"Ugh," she goes.

I wipe my eyes and sit up too. "What is it?"

"Nightmare."

I hug her but she pulls away slightly.

"You had no face, Jack."

"Shit."

I rub her back.

"It's okay Ally, it's just a nightmare. The faceless hasn't got me yet. Go back to sleep, you need your rest."

"Okay."

We lie back down in silence for a while, until Ally speaks softly.

"I keep thinking that doors going to open and the Faceless is going to come in."

I start stroking her curly hair. "Not going to happen. I'm your shrine remember. Go back to sleep."

Eventually Ally's breathing changes and I can tell she's fallen asleep.

I lie there in her soft warmth, wondering about the Faceless myself until I drift off to sleep too.

* * * * *

Early in the morning a rooster crowing wakes us up but we go back to sleep. Light filters through the cracked windows but we sleep in, until Ally wakes me by kissing my face all over and we have sex.

Breakfast is stolen —dry Nutri-grain from Riley's bus shrine and one warm energy drink shared between us.

It's a perfect start to the day and I can't help but think something is going to go wrong, like it always does every time we get a moment of relief.

"We need more food," says Ally, spooning up her last bit of dry cereal.

"There's an IGA in the middle of town I say we hit."

"Hang on. We haven't even checked this place out. There could be stuff in the main house."

"True. Should we have a look now?"

Ally nods and we exit the building.

Outside the morning sun filters through the birches and lights up the frost covered grass in the most beautiful way.

The main house is old and decrepit, with rusted metal and flaky white paint covering it. The door's locked, but with Ally's crowbar it's no trouble.

Inside is cluttered and gloomy. I take the torch from my pocket and flick it on.

The kitchen is a mess, like someone had been through here a long time ago.

We check the cupboards and the fridge but there's nothing for us, unless we wanted to eat cat-food.

I poke my head into the living room, just out of curiosity, and I'm delighted.

There at the round table is another card, and not only that, there's an old fiddle too, a mandolin and a guitar.

"No way."

Ally's at my side grinning beautifully. "How's that Jack! It's your lucky day!"

The Celts' restores my memories in a way that no card has done yet.

My family tree branches out before me. I see Mum playing the fiddle, then my Grandparents playing their instruments. Images flash through my mind of relatives I've never even met, on and on, up the family tree, until I'm somewhere else.

I see the white cliffs of Moher in Ireland and the traditional music of my heritage surges in my ears.

By the time I give the card to Ally I'm lost for words.

"A good one?"

"The best yet. I saw my ancestors. I heard them playing. *I saw Ireland.*"

Ally feels my joy as if its her own, and gives me a big hug. "You gonna play that fiddle for me?"

I grin. "Fuck yeah I am."

I take it up, spend a good minute getting it back in tune, then strike up a jig.

It feels like forever since I played, but my fingers remember their old tricks, even if they're a bit sluggish on the strings.

I stamp my foot against the floorboards to the beat and Ally starts bouncing around the room dancing, jumping up on the table.

We are both so happy. I don't want the moment to end, but it eventually we have to go.

*****

The IGA in Cygnet is a bust. It's already been completely raided. When we step out onto the street I say to Ally, "Back to the car?"

It's parked around the corner, just off the main road and out of sight from any renegades passing through.

Ally shakes her head. "We still need food. And I want some clean clothes. Isn't there a hippy shop up the road?"

"I think so."

We walk up Mary Street, invisible to the shades around us, but I see Ally glancing around nervously. Thankfully they all have faces.

We hold hands, even though we don't need to, and the hippy shop is only a short walk away.

Inside is as you would expect. Racks of bohemian clothing, crystals, decks of tarot cards, incense — all that usual hippy shop stuff.

A shade in all-black stands behind the counter.

I quietly walk to the far corner of the room and spark my light, just for a second.

The shade twitches up, then drifts straight out the door like it just knocked off.

Ally's already flicking through the racks of women's clothing. She grins and pulls out a beautiful patterned dress.

"Look Jack, isn't it nice?"

I smile at her. "Try it on," and she strips right in the middle of the store.

Perks of the apocalypse, right?

She looks ridiculously beautiful, sections of the patterns matching the red of her hair, her cleavage and unshaven legs on glorious display.

"Jesus Christ, Ally."

She grins. "You like?"

"Shit yeah."

"Just missing one thing."

"What's that?"

"This."

Ally smashes a nearby glass display cabinet and pinches a necklace. She puts it over her head, fixes her messy hair over the chain and smiles.

The green of the stone matches the colour of her eyes perfectly.

"You look like some kind of bohemian goddess."

"No, no, I'm an Empress of Fire remember?"

"Haha, you're right. The Empress of Fire."

I pull the most beautiful woman in the world into my arms and kiss her with so much intensity you'd think there was a flaming park bench beside us.

We stay in the hippy shop for a while. Ally decks me out in a full-on bohemian costume and she fills a bag with spare clothes.

As we go to leave, through the glass of the door I spot the renegade's ute cruising down the Mary Street.

"They're here."

Ally sees them too. "Shit. They must be looking for us Jack."

"It's okay, I don't think they saw us. We should bail now though, cut past the school and the top of the park."

"Alright. But they're in this area. We should pack up our shrine and hit the road again. If we stay another night the Faceless will rock up. I'm sure of it."

* * * * *

We sneak back to the car without seeing the renegades again, and I feel better now that we are back to the rifle.

I drive us out of town and to the house where we made the shrine and found *The Celts'* card.

We pack everything up, sleeping bags, the shrine, the boundary line, everything we brought. I also nick the fiddle from the house and chuck it in the boot of the Corolla.

I'm driving again, and I floor it wherever I can, trying to put as much distance between the renegades in their ute as possible.

We're cruising along the highway between Cygnet and Huonville when I spot someone walking along the side of the road.

I hit the brakes.

"What is it?" asks Ally.

I point, "Someone's walking."

But as we approach we see that it's not someone, but rather, something.

They're tall, dressed in full-black, walking slowly but deliberately. Where their face should be there's nothing. No eyes, no mouth, no nose, just smooth skin, all pale and framed by long and greasy black hair.

"Fuck," says Ally. "It's walked all the way from Hobart after us."

"What do we do? Just drive past it?"

"I don't know. It's just going to keep following us."

The Faceless is still a good distance away, and by now I've stopped the car completely.

"We shoot it?"

Ally nods. "We at least try. There aren't any other shades around. We might not get another chance."

We get out, I leave the car running, and Ally takes the rifle out of the back seat.

She flicks the bolt back, checks the chamber, and then gets ready to shoot, resting the barrel over the car.

I can't help but wish there was more time to appreciate the image of her standing there in that dress aiming the gun, her red hair blowing in the wind.

CRACK

The bullet connects. Straight in the chest of the Faceless, making it stumble for a second.

But apart from that the gunshot does nothing. It just keeps walking toward us with the same slow but deliberate pace as before.

"Another shot?"

Ally shakes her head. "We've only got two left. I don't think it's working. We have to save our ammo for fuckwits in utes. Any ideas?"

I reach for the lighter around my neck.

"You get close to it you die."

"Do you think the Faceless One is a bit thirsty after all that walking? Maybe it wants some Gatorade?"

Ally's eyes light up.

"Genius. We pour it on the ground in a big circle and bait the fucker into it."

"First we need to back the car up though."

"On it."

I grab the Gatorade bottle out of Ally's bag and back up too, following her as she reverses our Corolla further down the road.

She keeps going and I stop, unscrew the lid, then pour two thirds of the Gatorade bottle out in a circle on the road.

The smell of petrol fills my nose. I take off my talisman.

The Faceless continues to walk towards me, and soon Ally is by my side.

Static fills my ears, like that time I was in the New Sydney Hotel with the bugged card, and I can't hear what Ally's saying. Whispering in the voices of my loved ones torments me.

Ally grabs my hand, the ribbons of her talisman entwined with her fingers. She's holding the petrol, I'm holding the lighter talisman.

The Faceless One comes closer.

"This is it, Jack."

It steps into the ring of petrol on the road.

I know this could kill me but fuck it — I bend down, still holding Ally's hand, and light it up with the red BIC.

Whoosh

The static and deafening whispering changes. There's a piercing screech, and Ally throws the Gatorade bottle into the flames.

Then everything goes quiet. So quiet I can no longer hear a single thing, like all the sound was sucked out of the world.

I look to Ally. The red light of the fire bathes her. Everything seems to slow down for a second, then we hear this crackling sound like popcorn coming from the fire.

All of a sudden it's windy as hell — enough to nearly knock Ally and I over.

The flames blow wildly then go out completely, leaving nothing but a single tarot card swaying haphazardly in the wind.

Everything goes still.

The card falls to the ground and Ally turns to me.

"That actually worked."

"That was insane."

"Wonder what the card is?"

I'm about to say something when I hear the sound of an engine in the distance.

Ally turns to face the noise.

Coming from Cygnet is the white ute from before.

"Our car!"

We start sprinting.

"Get the gun, Ally."

ELEVEN

"**G**et the gun, Ally!"

The ute hurtles towards our car but we reach it first, Ally diving into the backseat after the rifle.

We do what we did before and get behind the Corolla while Ally aims.

But the ute doesn't slow right down like it did before.

For a moment I think they're going to ram us but the renegades go past.

They stop where we killed the shade and the girl that tried to hold us up in the IGA jumps out and swipes the tarot card.

"Fuck! Get the wheel Jack! We need that card!"

Frantically we take to the car and I floor it, making us lurch back against the seats.

"Seatbelts!"

We chase the ute through Woodstock, flying down the highway at well over a hundred.

"What do we do Ally?"

"Umm."

She flicks the bolt of the rifle back.

"Get close enough and I'll crack a shot at their tyre."

"You really think you can hit that?"

"I'm a good shot. I think I must've grown up around guns or something. I don't know what else to do."

"Okay but we've only got two shots left remember."

Ally grits her teeth, rolls down the window, making her hair blow everywhere like crazy.

My heart races as I speed through the countryside with the back of the renegade's ute in my sight.

I take the corners at breakneck speed and nearly slide off the road, but I get us close.

We're tailgating the ute when Ally climbs, half in the car half out of it, the rifle in her hands.

But the renegade fucks brake-check us, and Ally nearly falls out of the car.

"Shit!"

I give them more distance, thinking how dangerous this is.

But Ally is straight back at it, her top half out the car aiming the rifle at the ute's wheel.

"Closer!"

I press the accelerator down further.

CRACK!

I brake and Ally gets back into her seat.

"I think I hit it!"

She did.

The ute ahead slows and sparks fly from the back-left wheel. We hit a corner and the vehicle slides, braking hard and hitting the barrier but not with enough force to go through it.

I slam on the brakes and stop our car a stone's throw away from theirs.

Ally reloads the chamber.

"It's a stick-up."

"One shot."

We get out of the car and walk over, Ally aiming the rifle.

The renegades get out of the car, two blokes, the mean looking chick and the mousy girl that tried to roll us at the IGA in South Hobart. I see knives, a bat and a crowbar.

They're half-dazed from the crash and one stumbles. Ally and I press forward but we keep our distance.

Her finger is on the trigger. I'm holding Cass's wolf knife.

"Give us the card and no one gets shot!"

The renegades move closer to us.

"Stop where you are!"

The mean looking chick pulls out the card, steps closer to Ally.

They extend it forward, offering.

All at once.

She ducks down and drops the card, reaching for the end of Ally's rifle.

But Ally is the Empress of Fire.

She leaps back.

CRACK!

Blood. Screaming. Swearing.

Ally snaps the bolt back, pretending to reload the chamber.

"Get the fucking card Jack."

I do exactly as I'm told.

The renegades are in a total state of shock, two of them huddled over the chick that got shot and one of the blokes standing off against Ally with a crowbar. He calls her a, "Ranga Slut," as I pick up the tarot card.

I don't hear what Ally's saying because memories of my time spent on Maria Island surge through my mind.

'The Holiday.'

My massive family would go every year and a huge pack of us children would roam around together. For a moment I can see that white beach and those huge pine trees.

After the brief pause I move quickly to Ally's side and we back away to our car.

We say nothing to each other as we get in, myself taking the wheel.

I drive past the car crash, and the renegades watch as we go.

For a while the only sound is the car.

I look over and Ally has tears streaming down her face.

She turns to me, her face streaked with tears and speaks softly.

"I love you, Jack."

TWELVE

By the time I'm driving us up the Southern Outlet Ally is asleep in her seat, the rifle resting between her legs.

I feel less worried about her now, but she took the shooting badly.

So much happened so fast.

We arrive at Hobart, and I wake her before I turn onto Fitzroy Place.

But we find no relief here. There's a shade loitering inside the gate, within the boundary line.

"My shrine."

Ally goes to unbuckle her seatbelt but I still her hand.

"Could be a trap. Probably a trap."

Ally looks like she might cry again. I take my foot off the brake and we start rolling down the street.

I don't know what to do but I can't ask much of Ally right now.

"I like the road anyway."

Sniffle

"Wanna go to Maria Island? The card showed me memories there."

"Okay."

"The Fern Tree bus was running the day I started. If we leave now we can get to Triabunna by dark and get the ferry across tomorrow."

* * * * *

After a massive drive I stop at an old farmhouse just outside Triabunna. Ally and I shrine the barn and make a bed. She passes out within a minute of lying down.

My Empress is exhausted.

I watch her chest rise and fall with the smell of old hay filling my nose. Her face has softened since she fell asleep, and in the low light of a single tea-candle I can see tear-streak lines running down from her eyes.

Only a few hours ago she was bluffing a group of killers with an empty gun.

* * * * *

The next morning we finish off the Nutri-Grain and pack up the shrine. Triabunna is only a short drive away and we park the car at some random house around the corner from the jetties so it's out of sight.

Ally seems better today. We both got a good sleep and I feel optimistic.

We lock the car and walk. I carry our bags and Ally carries the rifle, her talisman hanging from her wrist. She's still wearing the dress from the hippy shop and the green crystal necklace. I'm still wearing the mental bohemian costume she dressed me in.

I laugh. "We'd look so funny in the real world."

Ally laughs too. "Just a hippy couple on a road trip going to Maria with a gun."

"Should've brought a camera to get a photo with the wombats!"

"Nah, we just brought a bit of petrol instead. You know, to get a few marshmallows going."

We both laugh, maybe a bit too loud. Then the laughter fades, leaving only the sound of our boots on the gravel. Shades loiter further up the street, no longer seeming so dangerous after everything that's happened, but still a reminder of where we are.

Alt Tasmania. Tarot Limbo. The apocalypse.

I squeeze Ally's hand tighter. We just keep walking, heads down, like a couple of tourists who took the wrong turn into hell but decided to see it through anyway.

The jetty comes into view and the ferry sits on the water there with the island stretching long and low across the horizon behind it.

This feels big.

I'm ready for something to go wrong. But Maria feels steady with memories of my childhood and knowing that they came from killing the Faceless One. It's like we were meant to come here.

Ally holds the rifle with the butt of the gun in her hand and the barrel resting on her shoulder. With her other hand she takes her talisman off it — her madman's rosary — Cass's incomplete deck, the binder clips, rings and ribbons — and entwines her fingers, then mine with it.

We don't have to say anything.

We're a walking shrine with both our talismans and Ally's bag full of charms and packed up shrine.

Shades mill about at the ferry terminal. Some drift onto the boat and so do we, silent the whole time.

We go upstairs and go towards the bow to sit and wait.

We've seen a few shades aboard already but there are none of them up here.

It's nice to sit.

The sea-breeze blows Ally's hair and seagulls squawk for chips from a group of guys wearing sunglasses in the distance.

All of a sudden, we are moving.

* * * * *

Bishop and Clerk hulks in the distance, the dolerite crag-ged-mountain top against a backdrop of Australia's crackling blue sky.

The familiar convict buildings and ruins grow close, and so does the white sandy beach and bush.

The old cement silos loom as we approach the jetty and I see shades walking on the island but they're outnumbered by the wildlife. Geese, wombats, pademelons, kangaroos — they're everywhere here.

Ally squeezes my hand when the boat docks.

"This is us."

"Maria Island."

We wait for a few shades to leave before drifting off the boat and onto the jetty.

I half expect for something to suddenly go wrong, but the sea smells sharp, gullshit stains the jetty and for a second it's just Maria. I remember jumping off this jetty with my cousins even though it's freezing cold in the water here.

I'm pulled out of the moment when we set foot on real ground before the silos and spot a small shrine of cairn stones, feathers, shells, driftwood and rusted convict relics. The boundary around it forms a circle like a fairy ring, a few metres across.

Ally readies her gun and starts looking around the place.

My heart races as I'm instantly thrown into fight or flight.

"Put it down please!"

Someone stands up from the slope and we see they're carrying a rifle but not pointing it at us.

Ally just freezes, aiming at the person.

They're a man in their thirties, tall and solidly built. The expression on their face looks calm.

I yell out. "It's empty!"

Ally turns to me, "What are you doing, Jack?"

"Not here. Not on Maria." Then I yell back to the stranger. "We're friendly, the rifle is for self-defence!"

The man nods, swings his gun over his shoulder, and walks down the slope towards us.

Ally looks to me and I can see how on edge she is.

"I hope you're right about this."

The stranger offers his hand.

"Name's Dom."

"I'm Jack. This is Ally."

"I must've given yous a fright. Sorry."

The man's gruff but I get a sense he means us no harm.

"We're used to frights. Don't worry about it."

Dom nods. "You've been *out there*. How long?"

I look to Ally, she's silent and tense. I do the talking.

"Me, a couple weeks. Her —a few months. Are there others here?"

Dom smiles. "A whole community. Come to the Mess Hall in Darlington with me, protocol is a meeting with everyone to decide what to do with new arrivals."

He sets off along the gravel road and we follow, Ally clutching her rifle and lingering a half pace behind.

I clear my throat. "How many?"

"Twenty-two. Kids, rangers, old people. Some started here, others were led here by memory."

I glance at Ally, her mouth is tight and she doesn't say anything.

"How do you stay safe from the shades with that many people? How many shrines do you have on the Island?"

Dom chuckles a little. "'Shades?' 'Shrines?' — I like those. Never knew what to call the fuckers. If I know what you mean by shrine then you two look like a walking one — look at yous. We do community art projects to keep them out of our safe areas. When them 'shades' come and add their pieces we take them away. We've set the perimeter up with multiple art projects in layers for extra protection."

"That's smart. We never thought of layering them. How big is the boundary?"

"All of Darlington."

My jaw drops. "All of Darlington? How long have your people been here?"

By now we're coming out of the pines and crossing the bridge.

"Some have been here for twenty years."

I catch another glance at Ally

I think I see a glimmer of hope in her eyes.

Their boundary lines come into view. Before the cluster of convict buildings are cairn stone stacks with feathers, driftwood, rusted convict artefacts, animal bones and shells.

The sheer scale of it blows my mind. I wonder what Ally's thinking.

There at the boundary we see the first other survivor.

It's an old fella and I can hear the tune he's singing as he's stacking cairn stones from here.

'Over the road with me pack on me back

Over the road with me big heavy sack

Holes in me shoes and me toes peepin' through

Sing skidderi dill doodle dam it's only Johnny Doo—"

He's singing the 'Little Beggarman,' and looks up to see us and smiles.

The smell of Maria Island, that twang of sea mingled with animal shit swims in my nose. Nostalgia washes over me.

I feel like I'm coming home.

*****

We sit in the Mess Hall, where convicts once gathered for meals and prayer and learning.

Now we gather, Ally and I standing before a mixed audience. I see warm faces and soft eyes. All ages. Some watch us cautiously, eyeing Ally's rifle, others smile and one of the kids, one wearing a talisman of feathers around their neck, is gleefully pointing at Ally's red hair like they've never seen that colour before.

Their leader, "Maureen," or "Mo," as they call her, is a wiry woman in her sixties. An ex-schoolteacher. She does most of the talking, in a no nonsense kind of way, and I can immediately see why everyone respects her.

"You're fighters. I can tell she's had to use that rifle."

Ally goes still.

"It was a life-or-death situation," I explain.

"I wanted to hear it from her."

I nod and look to Ally. For a moment she just stands there silent, her chest tight. Then.

"We had just taken care of a Faceless One when these renegades came back for us."

Mo just nods. That's enough of an explanation for her.

One of the other survivors chimes in, a park ranger whose voice seems to hold some weight.

"You killed one of the nofaces?"

I nod and reach for my lighter tether. "My tie to the real world. We used some petrol too."

Someone in the room says, "You bring that kind of fight here, we all go under."

The room murmurs, half with us half against us.

Mo's eyes widen slightly and she leans forward. "And it worked because that lighter is special to you?"

"It belongs to my best friend. We're trying to get it back to him."

"Renegades, Faceless, collecting cards," begins Dom. "They might be useful Mo."

"We can't risk it," someone says.

"But they came all this way," says the old fella who was singing little beggarman.

Mo shakes her head. "We didn't last this long turning away those in need." She eyes Ally cautiously, then me. "You've been *out there*. You made it *here*. That counts for something. But trust on Maria isn't given cheap."

"You'll stay in the penitentiary. You'll eat with us. You'll help with the work. In the end we'll decide whether you belong here or not."

* * * * *

The next few days pass by like a dream. Work, faces, fragments of the old world. Trust.

Ally and I sleep in our own room in the old convict penitentiary. There the fireplace keeps us warm at night and we sleep in bags on the wooden bunks. In the mornings we join the others, hauling wood for fires, driftwood for shrines and cairn stones for boundary lines.

There's laughter sometimes, and at first it feels strange after weeks of constant dread, but I soon get used to it.

Ally not so much.

She drifts between her silence and fire. One moment I'm watching her paint cairn stones with ochre, helping a little girl to crush the pigment with a soft patience I've only ever glimpsed at — the next she's staring out at the water holding her rifle, her eyes locked on the ferry and shades arriving.

The others notice, and don't say anything, but I can feel it. Dom finds excuses to work near us and I think it's to keep an eye out for trouble. Every glance is a test.

Soon the rhythm of Maria begins to pull us in.

* * * * *

On the third night we find 'The Group' card in our cabin.

It restores memories of my childhood on Maria — gallivanting around with a pack of brothers and cousins, climbing trees and playing 'nut wars', card game tournaments of 'spit', beating on the invasive thistles with sticks.

Ally smiles. "Six and a half left."

"I wonder how many more are on the island."

Her smile drops. "That might be the only one."

I can tell what she's thinking. Eventually we have to leave.

That's when there's a knocking on the door.

"It's Dom — Mo wants to see yous."

We walk along the verandah to the mess hall.

Inside Mo is waiting, with a senior group of islanders sitting around in chairs. We take a seat.

She gets straight to the point. "Jack and Ally. We've decided you can stay as long as you like. But in exchange we need your help."

Ally and I look to each other. She shakes her head. I explain.

"We won't stay too long. We have to get back out there and complete my tarot deck. This place makes me miss the real world even more."

Mo nods. "Do as you please. We are still asking for your help. You've said after you killed the shade and the Faceless One arrived, your tether and some petrol was enough to put it down?"

I look to Ally and see her jaw locked.

"You want to clear the shades off the island don't you? But you need to be able to kill the Faceless that show up on the next ferry too."

Mo nods. "With your lighter, our gas, and the right plan. Could it be done?"

I'm surprised when Ally speaks before I do.

"We'll do it."

* * * * *

Boots and the sound of the trolley wheels on gravel. Petrol sloshing in the drums.

Mo barks orders in the distance and we cross the boundary out of Darlington where a group of kids sit painting cairn stones.

We wheel the trolleys over the bridge and under the pine trees. There we leave one with the other survivors, then Ally, Dom and I push the other all the way down to the jetty.

The ferry has just arrived. Perfect timing.

We dump the trolley at the end of the jetty, then enact the next phase of the plan.

I take off my talisman and pass it to Ally.

Standing there on the jetty with the shades all around I am completely exposed.

Perfect.

"Come and get me you seedy bastards!"

Heads turn and I bolt for the ringed boundary line and shrine where the jetty meets the land.

Static fills my ears, and the sound of my heart pounding, but I'm not afraid.

Ally and Dom keep their distance and watch as shade after shade bugs the boundary line around me.

The items stick out like sore thumbs against the artistry of the islanders and I pick them apart easily, tossing them a few metres away from the boundary.

When the last bug lands I swipe it and all the others around me and piss bolt.

Deafening static and satanic voices fill my ears.

Ally runs alongside me and puts my talisman over my head.

"You okay?" she asks as the shades chase after us.

Our boots grate against the gravel.

"Better now."

"Here, pass me some bugs."

We arrive under the pine trees to see Mo and the other survivors standing around a small shrine and boundary line that wasn't there before. Right next to it is a drum of petrol, the charmed-up rangers ute parked nearby.

"It's a go!" yells Dom.

Mo nods and barks orders for the survivors to pour petrol while Ally and I surge forth with hands full of bugs and shades chasing after us.

We dump them on the shrine, jump in the ute, and everyone else scatters.

Dom's driving and Ally and I are in the tray pouring a trail of petrol behind us.

Everything is tense, but we drive slowly, watching as shades begin gathering under the pines, drawn to the bugged shrine in the middle of the road.

We reach our destination, another newly made shrine and boundary line, just on the other side of the bridge, and get out of the ute.

Shades from all over the island are drawn in. They stand around the bugged shrine in a big mob, and the more that come, the more bugs they bring, until eventually an entire horde is gathered under the eaves of the giant convict pine trees.

Mo gives me the signal.

I lean down and spark the petrol on the ground with my lighter.

The flames whoosh down in a trail, across the bridge and under the feet of the shades.

There's a split second where nothing happens.

BOOM!

The explosion makes my ears ring and I feel the shock-wave in my chest.

The pine trees burn and the shades with them.

"An hour till the next ferry," says Dom, rattling his keys. "Get in and hold on, it's a bumpy ride to get to the other bridge."

* * * * *

The ferry approaches the jetty and Dom, Ally and I handle the petrol drums together, dousing the jetty while the Faceless mob watch from on deck.

They step off and we run, leaving a trail behind us like a fuse.

The air crackles with static. I see Mo and some of the other survivors watching from the silos

I hold Ally's talisman entwined-hand and take off the lighter necklace.

"Your turn."

My breath catches as she lights the trail of petrol.

Whoosh

The jetty goes up and Faceless Ones crackle like popcorn in the inferno.

Ally squints, her face bathed in red light.

"Fuck. There's still two on the boat."

I see them. Two blank faces staring out the window.

I pull a deodorant can out of my jacket pocket.

A gale wind blows out the flames on the jetty.

"Where?" asks Ally.

"It was rattling around in the ute."

The Faceless step off the boat and drift down the jetty. I shake up the aerosol can and give it to Ally.

"Enter: The Empress of Fire."

* * * * *

We find five more tarot cards in the process of leaving Maria Island. Two are dropped by the pair of faceless Ally flamethrowered, one was found in the ashes of the pines, another on the ferry, and the last one at the barn on the hill where we said goodbye to the islanders for good in the light of a sunset.

Ally and I get off the ferry at Triabunna at dusk. We walk back to the car without incident.

"At least now we've got some music," replies Ally.

"What?"

"That Dom guy gave me a mixtape – some dead twenty-something's mixtape. I think he said his name was Ned. Used to play fiddle around Hobart apparently. Do you know him?"

"No idea. What's on it?"

"See for yourself."

The CD reads:

1. *Day One – Rura*
2. *Vampire Empire – Adrianne Lenker*
3. *Drive – Greta Ray*
4. *Closer – Jack River*
5. *All My Friends – LCD Soundsystem*
6. *Hell & Back – Sticky Fingers*
7. *Wide Open Road – Carla Geneve*
8. *Circle the Drain – Soccer Mommy*
9. *Seventeen – Sharon Van Etten*
10. *Bittersweet Symphony – The Verve*

11. *Los Angeles – Big Thief.*

12. *See You Free – Bonny Light Horsemen*

"I can't actually remember if I know any of these songs."

"Probably just some weirdo's music. Dom said it was his tether, and he fell off Bishop & Clerk."

Ally sighs.

"Just a hippy couple on a road trip coming back from Maria with a gun."

"*Shit.* We didn't get a photo of a wombat."

THIRTEEN

"Home sweet home."

Headlights off. Darkness.

"Home sweet trap."

We both laugh, but then the laughter goes hollow. I look to Ally.

"We really going in?"

"Could be the last card."

"Could be the end."

Ally's smile cuts through the night.

"Trial by fire."

I kill the engine. We get out, Ally with the empty rifle, her talisman dangling from her wrist.

The gate creaks and the boundary line running on the inside of the fence has been desecrated.

Ally and I exchange a look but don't say anything. She jerks the barrel of her gun towards the front door.

I take our keys out of my pocket, but the door is already unlocked.

I glance at Ally quickly, she's aiming the rifle at the door, I push it open.

The shrine's been kicked in, the place is a mess.

Ally whispers, *"They've been here."*

A match flares in the dark.

Riley's eyes glint with flame.

"Nice place. Thought I'd move in."

Ally flicks on the lights and we see what he's done to the place.

Her paintings are trashed. The cracked-teapot shrine is shattered.

I hold Cass's knife up my jacket sleeve, but Riley must see it poking out because he says, "Nice apple-peeler. I brought my own toy to play with."

He laughs.

Riley pulls out a notched machete.

"This. This is my tether."

Ally jabs the barrel of the rifle at him.

"Drop it or I'll shoot."

Riley's face goes blank. Then he smiles.

"If you had any ammo left."

Ally flicks the bolt back, pretending to load a round into the chamber.

"I know the sound of an empty gun. My empty gun."

"Time to go, Ally."

Riley steps closer and Ally locks her aim onto him, her whole body tense.

He's going to go for her.

I lunge forward with Cass's knife.

Riley laughs and leaps back.

CRACK

Before I even see it he's pulled out a pistol and fired a shot at our feet. We freeze, ears ringing, and Riley grins.

"Tethers, talisman, cards, all your shit. The car. And I'm taking the girl this time."

Ally holds the rifle like a club. "You're dreaming!"

Riley aims the pistol at my legs.

BANG, BANG, BANG, on the door.

"OPEN UP!"

Riley hesitates for a split second.

Ally hurls the rifle at him with a wild look in her eyes.

I dive forth with Cass's knife.

Ally's throw connects, enough to cut the distance without getting shot.

I'm swinging Cass's knife and she's at my side with one of her palette knives in hand.

We dive at Riley like a couple of serial killers and total mayhem ensues.

My knife misses.

Riley lifts his pistol.

Ally stabs him in the shoulder with a palette knife and he drops it.

"BITCH!"

CRASH

The light flickers and the door caves in.

Riley reels back and smashes me across the jaw with the handle of his machete.

Everything goes white. I hit the floor.

When I look up Riley has Ally pressed against the wall, his machete under her chin.

"Aren't we going to have fun together."

Static fills the room. I glance at the door and see three shades standing there — cops wearing sunglasses and gloves.

They come forth with arms reaching towards me.

I clutch my lighter at the ready.

All of a sudden Riley is there, cleaving at the shades with his machete while Ally and I watch in shock.

Shades scream. Static erupts like the room is full of broken radios.

The windows shatter and more of them swarm the room.

Chaos.

We fight with our tethers. I give Ally the knife. Riley swings his machete. I torch shades with the lighter around my neck and an aerosol can.

Fire. Blood. Swearing.

Shades scream and crackle like popcorn.

One moment Riley is cutting down a shade that's reaching for Ally, the next he's shoving me into one.

I barely hold onto my life.

Riley clears a window.

"Good luck!"

And then he's gone, leaving Ally and I alone in her trashed living room with a crowd of shades.

I torch one of them, blasting them in their sunglasses-covered face with my makeshift flamethrower.

"We gotta bail!"

Ally plunges Cass's knife into a shade. "You think?!"

I burn one that's climbing through the window, then shove Ally through it.

Glass cuts my skin as I dive through after her, cold hands trying to grasp my ankles. I tumble onto the pavers.

Ally stands over me, knifes an all-black, then pulls me to my feet.

Together we vault over the fence onto Fitzroy Place.

I'm running for the car, hand in hand with Ally, when she pulls me back and points with her hand holding the knife.

A small pack of shades walk down the street carrying bugs, headed in the direction Riley must've gone.

Ally looks to me with fire in her eyes.

"We have to finish this."

FOURTEEN

We're walking up Wentworth Street in South Hobart when the shades carrying bugs turn and disappear up a driveway.

I glance behind us.

In the distance is a whole pack of them. I used my lighter to ward them off earlier but they still follow.

Some have no faces.

Ally pauses. "This is it Jack. We go in. He's not coming out."

I grit my teeth.

"Whatever happens — I love you, Ally."

"I love you too, Jack."

We walk up the overgrown driveway. At the top is a boundary line stacked with wallaby skulls and cracked pairs of sunglasses.

The shades ahead of us plant their bugs, then turn back down the driveway. We pass by them like we're invisible and trash the boundary line, kicking away the charms and leaving the bugs.

Ally and I press on.

The house we find has gone to shit. The garden's overgrown, the paint's peeling and the corrugated iron roof is sagging.

This is it.

Ally whispers, *"Not the front door."*

We go around the side of the house.

Everything is dark and silent, aside from the whisperings of the shades climbing the driveway.

Ally and I find the backdoor.

It's unlocked and we open it gently but the rusted hinges still creak.

The two of us exchange a look, then venture into the dark.

Inside is much like the out — rundown and grotty, the walls of the corridor are scratched and stained with old blood.

My heart races. We have no real plan. We're just a couple of artists trying to put down a killer.

Ally's nails dig into the back of my hand. She leads me on.

We reach the kitchen and see Riley's shrine sitting on the counter.

Propped up by a pile of animal skulls is a rusted bear trap, it's jaws frozen open and stained with blood. All around it are the broken sunglasses of dead shades.

He must've killed so many faceless.

As I'm thinking that I see something else on the counter.

I reach for the polaroid.

It's a photo of a Faceless One, the background full of hospital beds and machines. Then I see it.

In the hand of the Faceless is a tarot card that's been cut in half.

My card.

Creak

The door swings open and Riley stands in the gloom, machete in hand.

"Fancy seeing yous here."

He pulls out his pistol and aims it at me.

A faceless head looms over his shoulder.

Ally steps between me and the gun and shoves Riley back.

Static erupts. The faceless wraps one arm around Riley's chest and with its free hand it reaches for his face.

When the hand drops Riley stumbles forward then freezes, twitches, then he throws his head back and we see that where his face once was, there is only smooth skin.

I use the aerosol can with the lighter and spew flames all over Riley and the faceless behind him.

Crackle. Snap. Pop.

The ground shakes.

A card falls from the ceiling and Ally snatches it before grabbing my hand.

"Time to go, Jack."

FIFTEEN

I park our charmed-up Corolla out the front of the Royal Hobart Hospital and we get out, dressed like walking shrines in our bohemian outfits riddled with feathers and leaves and other trinkets.

I shake my lighter and read the barcode on the back.

Only a few good sparks left.

The hospital towers over us. Ally reaches for my hand, entwining the ribbons of her madman's rosary between my fingers. Her other hand holds Riley's machete. Mine holds our bag of tricks.

Shades drift in and out busily and I realise what we are about to walk into —a whole hive of them, most in uniform — eerie doctors and nurses with eyes unseen behind black sunglasses.

"There's heaps of machines in that picture," says Ally. "We should check cardio and ICU first."

I squeeze her hand. "Cardio is closer to the ground. Let's start there."

* * * * *

We creep through the ward.

All around us are machines humming with static and flickering lights.

Shadows dance as shades go about the different beds.

Ally and I prowl around the entire ward, hand-in-hand and wordless.

At last she shakes her head, then jerks Riley's machete toward the ceiling.

I nod and we leave, taking the stairs up to the ICU ward.

It's the same story here, only the air is colder.

We creep around one wing of the ward, round the corner, then see it.

The Faceless One stands at the end of the ward clutching half a tarot card. It's blank head flicks towards us as if it can see us and it starts walking.

I take the aerosol out of Ally's bag before swinging it over my shoulder.

But before the gap between us and the Faceless is closed, the other shades pause.

Heads turn. They notice us. All at once.

The whole ward flips out —lights flicker like it's some haunted rave, machines scream with static and doctors, nurses, patients and security start appearing from every direction.

Fuck.

A shade reaches for Ally and she cuts its arm clean off.

Two more come up behind her and I torch them.

But for every shade we kill, there's three more around the corner.

In the chaos, Ally loses the machete and we run for the stairwell, hitting it fast.

A horde climbs from below.

There's nowhere to run but up.

Our boots pound the stairs, up and up.

We're climbing and I slip, Ally's bag and her belongings fly everywhere.

"This'll do, Jack! Boundary line it!"

We scramble to arrange the charms and build a boundary and shrine across the stairwell. It's messy, but it'll allow us to isolate the Faceless from the other shades.

I grab the Gatorade bottle. We climb one more flight of stairs and hit the roof.

The buildings of Hobart trace against a skyline of dying sunset and looming mountain.

We run to the edge but there's nowhere to jump to.

I turn and pour petrol on the ground in a big circle.

The Faceless One steps out onto the rooftop.

"Psst, psst, psst. Here kitty-kitty," says Ally and I can't help but laugh despite everything.

But the Faceless doesn't want to step in the circle of petrol.

It follows us around the rooftop.

I try torch it with my makeshift flamethrower but the spark on my lighter is too weak.

I glance at the barcode as we back away towards the stairs.

000010

One more spark and I die.

One more spark and Fred dies.

The Faceless moves toward us.

Ally shoves me hard into the stairwell.

What the fuck Ally.

I'm thinking it but I can't say it.

Somehow I catch myself from rolling down them by clinging to the second step.

Cement cracks against my shins and scrapes my arms.

I peer over the top step to see Ally standing holding a huge nitrous oxide canister, the Faceless One getting closer by the second.

She holds her tether — the Redhead match burnt at the wrong end.

BOOM

Ally!

But when I climb up Ally is gone.

Only flames and burnt cement remained.

I see the other half of *'The Card-Cutter'* floating through the air.

The last card.

I just collapse outside the stairwell and weep.

Ally is dead.

SIXTEEN

*A*lly died saving me.

I wipe my face, blood, snot, sweat and tears makes my hands black and red.

My Empress of Fire.

I don't know why, but I paint her on the cement wall outside the stairwell as the tarot card.

My blood for Ally's curly red hair and eyes.

Ash mixed with my tears for the rest of her.

When I step back to look at it I feel dizzy.

I'm falling forwards, about to crack my head open on the wall.

Darkness.

* * * * *

Light.

Beeping.

I blink.

Someone is staring at me.

Fred.

It's Fred! His face lights up when he sees I'm awake.

Fred crushes me with a hug.

"Jack! Jack's awake!"

I'm in a hospital bed, attached to machines.

Sunshine filters through clean glass windows.

"What happened to me?" I rasp.

"You've been in a coma for three weeks man. Doctor! We need a doctor!"

"It's alright Fred, I'm fine."

Something is in my hand.

I offer Fred his red BIC, with the sticker torn and safety removed.

"Don't lose it bro. It's a good lighter."

"How the fuck do you have that?"

"I borrowed it for a while. It saved my life. It's yours."

Fred gives it a spark. The flame dances, then goes out without him taking his finger off the button.

The lighter runs out.

I'm alive.

Everything shifts as the Doctor arrives. They're checking my vitals.

A nurse pops around the curtain, sunglasses hanging out her pocket.

"Erin's awake too."

"Ally!"

Everyone looks at me confused.

"She said Erin, bro."

"Red hair, green eyes, crack shot with a rifle."

The doctor pauses.

I stare. I must look crazy.

"That's her. Is she holding a burnt match?"

The nurse looks like she's just seen a ghost.

The curtain flies open.

Messy red hair.

Hospital gown, wires dangling.

Electric look on her face.

My heart splits into pieces.

"I'm sorry I pushed you down a flight of stairs!"

I laugh and cry at the same time.

"Ally!"

To the absolute bewilderment of everyone else, she dives into my arms before anyone can stop her.

Ally smells like home and smoke, and she has tiny pieces of ash all through her hair.

I found her.

My Empress of Fire.